I0589616

Astrobia

A Sonny and Breanne Mystery
(Book 3)

A Novel by
James C. Paavola

Published by J&M Book Publishers
Memphis, Tennessee

www.jamespaavola.com

ISBN: 978-0-9964571-8-7

Printed in the United States of America

ALSO BY JAMES PAAVOLA

A Sonny and Breanne Mystery series:
Call Me Firefly
Jack and the Beanpole

Murder In Memphis series:
The Unspeakable
(A 2018 Killer Nashville Silver Falchion Finalist)
Cast the First Stone
Blood Money
Which One Dies Today?
They Gotta Sleep Sometime
The Chartreuse Envelope

Short stories in the *Malice in Memphis* anthologies
edited by Carolyn McSparren:

Heinous Crimes and Murder
In *Torn Letters* (expected early 2021)

A Cry from the Ashes
In *Mayhem in Memphis* (2019)

Down in the Furnace Room:
A Sonny and Breanne Mystery
In *Elmwood: Stories to Die For* (2017)

The Adventures of Sonny Etherly: Special Powers
In *Ghost Stories* (2016)

The Silver Star
In *Bluff City Mysteries* (2014)

Acknowledgements

I want to thank my core team: my wife Marilyn for her support and proof reading, our daughter Shannon for her creativity in crafting the cover, and Carolyn McSparren for her detailed editing of the manuscript.

Thanks also to our critique group—Phyllis Appleby, Barbara Christopher, Carolyn McSparren, and Patricia Potter—for their learned reviews and encouragement. Thanks so much.

The Sonny and Breanne mystery novels were inspired by characters I introduced in two short stories published by Dark Oak Press—*The Adventures of Sonny Elliott: Special Powers* (2016), and *Down in the Furnace Room: A Sonny and Breanne Mystery* (2017) .

Acknowledgements

DEDICATION

Joel David Paavola
9-16-71 to 6-4-18

In your short time with us, son,
you made an incredible difference in our lives
and in the lives of so many others.
There is a hole in our hearts.
We miss you so much.

One

Sonny

I hit ENTER.

Instantly, a piercing siren sounded.

I winced and covered my ears, then squinted at the screen. *Only fifty-three seconds 'till the keypad explodes.*

Hurry! I checked the coded message—**61905294**.

Argh. That siren's making my teeth vibrate. I can't think straight. The seconds ticked off.

42 seconds.

Concentrate. ... I don't see any pattern.

31 seconds.

I need four single-digit numbers for the passcode. Divide the coded message into four pairs: 61, 90, 52, 94.

23 seconds.

Add the numbers of each pair. 6+1=7, 9+0=9, 5+2=7, 9+4=13. That's 7, 9, 7, 13. Won't work. Thirteen's a two-digit number.

<u>11 seconds.</u>

Nothing there. Think!

The siren vibrated inside my head.

<u>3 seconds.</u>

"Breakfast's ready!"

Huh? I looked up. "Oh, no. Wait!"

BOOM!

The keypad exploded. Clouds of smoke filled the screen. A fiery sign appeared:

BETTER LUCK NEXT TIME SONNY ETHERLY

"Sonny! Whacha doin' up there?"

"Coming, Grams." I took one last look at the computer screen, then clomped down the stairs.

"I swan," said Grams. "I was callin' 'n callin'. Your computer's louder 'n me."

"Sorry. I was just playing a game."

"What kinda game?"

"It's called 'Code Breaker.' "

Grams made a face and shrugged.

"Like spy stuff. You know, spies leave messages in code. You have to figure out the code to get the message."

"Like they did in World War II?" she asked.

"Yeah. Battles were won or lost depending on which army could break the other army's code."

"You fixin' to join the Marines like your daddy? Or the Air Force like your momma, God rest her soul?"

I smiled. "No, ma'am. Not that coordinated or that brave. But I've seen ads for the CIA. They want people who are good at decoding."

"The CIA. Those the spies?"

I nodded. "Central Intelligence Agency. But the decoders aren't spies. They sit in a room with lots of computers trying to break the most complicated codes."

"You any good at it?"

"Not as good as I thought I was. I couldn't figure that last one out in time."

"That the big explosion I heard?"

I nodded.

"Any other eighth graders play that game?"

I shrugged. "Don't know."

Grams smiled. "Come 'n get you some breakfast. Maybe it'll sharpen your brain so you won't get exploded next time."

Two

Breanne

"Breanne Thurman!" Momma called from the foot of the stairs. "Need to get a move-on, young lady. You're going to be late for school."

"I'm coming, Momma," I yelled as I swung into my backpack. I grabbed my glasses and hurried down the steps.

Momma stuck out both hands—one holding a brown paper bag, the other a toasted sandwich half wrapped in a paper napkin.

I took the sandwich and leaned down to kiss Momma's cheek. Then I turned around so she could drop my lunch in the backpack. I took a bite of the sandwich as she zipped the backpack closed.

"Off with you now," Momma said, holding the door open. Have a good day at school. And don't forget to check your teeth in a mirror. That cheesy scrambled egg sandwich you're eating will get caught in your braces, big time."

I hurried down the porch steps to the sidewalk and turned right. I was more than halfway through my sandwich when I spotted a familiar figure walking a few blocks ahead—a black boy, much shorter than me, leaning under the weight of his bulging backpack. I stuffed the rest of the sandwich in my mouth and stretched out my long skinny legs. Caught up to him as he opened the school door.

"Hey, Sonny," I said, breathing heavily.

Sonny looked up. "Hey, Bree." He bounced his backpack to a more comfortable position. "I waited, but when you didn't come I went ahead on."

I patted Sonny's backpack. "Why've you got so many books in here? Looks like it's gonna split open."

"Library books for a history paper. Each day, Ms Case lets a few of us out of first period early to go to the school library. Today's my day. I'll turn these in and check out a few more."

"That reminds me, I have to go to the library, too. I did book reports on Alice in Wonderland *and* Through the Looking-Glass for language arts. Ms Hill wants me to do some extra credit research on 'alternative worlds' using those two stories as examples."

"Huh?"

"You're into science, right?" I asked. "You know about alternative worlds existing side-by-side, but neither world knows about the other."

"You talkin' about *string theory*? *String theory* says our universe is probably only one of a whole bunch of universes."

I didn't know what he was talking about. My mouth hung open.

Sonny made a face. "Eww! Gross. You been eatin' egg salad or something?"

Forgot to check my braces. I lowered my head and let my long hair hang down to hide my face. Then I used my tongue to clean the cheesy egg off my braces. I raised up and smiled. "Better?"

"It'll do."

"Thanks for telling me." I licked my braces again. "So what about stringy things?"

"String theory" he said. "It's physics."

"Physics?"

"Yeah. String theory says that Earth is part of a huge universe, but it's not the only universe. There are lots of other universes all around us that we can't see. They're called parallel universes. Each one with planets kinda like Earth. That planet and our planet would be parallel worlds."

"Parallel worlds? That's way more than I want to think about, Mr. Brainiac. Now back to my non-scientific, extra credit project. My different worlds are connected by secret passages."

"*Portals*," Sonny said. "Science calls those secret passages *portals*. Get it? The old Latin word for a city's large gate was 'portale.' So, portal means the way in and the way out. Like in the movies, spaceships are always jumping into *hyperspace* to get from one dimension to another, or from one world to another. Hyperspace is one kind of portal."

I rolled my eyes as big as I could. "Thank you for the over-the-top lesson in the meaning of words. Now, if I may continue... Alice found two *portals,*" I said with emphasis.

He smiled, and pushed his thick black-rimmed glasses up with his index finger.

"Two different portals into the world of Wonderland—one was a rabbit hole that Alice tumbled into, the other a mirror that she walked through."

"That Wonderland's a cool world—talking animals, a disappearing cat, marching playing cards, a smoking caterpillar—"

"Slow down," I interrupted. "This is *my* extra credit."

"How come you get to do extra credit?"

"Whataya talking about? You got extra credit for your project on rock formations when we were studying asteroids."

"True." Sonny looked over at me, cocked his head, then changed the subject. "So how come you were late this morning?"

I heard a shout and looked up to see two students running in and out of the crowded hall, coming right at us. "Let's talk silently."

Sonny nodded.

The boys zipped past us.

Got up late. I thought. *Didn't sleep so good knowing today just won't be the same.*

I read Sonny's mind. *I've been thinking the same thing. Gonna be boring without all the drama.*

You mean, without my worrying about getting beat up by Deena and her bully friends?

Their plan was to beat you up, then try to blame you for stealing the teacher's watch. Thank goodness our three ghost friends stopped them, kept you safe, and got Deena expelled.

Yeah. So cool to be protected by Ashni, Timmy and Luis.

He nodded. *It's good that our spirit friends were able to clear up their unfinished business on earth so they could cross over.*

I'm happy for them. It's just that we spent so much time together before they left. I miss them, especially Ashni.

Yup. Our last year of Middle school's gonna be boring without ghosts.

We took the stairs. Sonny left at the second floor, raised an open hand in a silent goodbye.

"See you second period," I said, and kept climbing to my locker on the third floor to drop my afternoon books. I ran my tongue across my braces a few more times, then joined the flow of kids hurrying to beat the tardy bell.

Three

Breanne

I was already sitting at our little table in the back of the cafeteria—the one the kids call the *nerd table*—when Sonny came up with his tray filled with food. He gave me his usual one-nod-up greeting, sat, and immediately shoved a heaping forkful of shepherd's pie into his mouth.

I held up a half sandwich with two bites out of it. "My mom packed my lunch."

And, just like Sonny, he began talking with his mouth full. "Aw ranges ang."

"I keep telling you. Don't talk with your mouth full. It's gross. Besides, I can't understand a word."

Sonny chewed some more, then swallowed hard. "I said, I was in the library and saw the strangest thing." He shoveled another forkful into his mouth, and started talking again.

"Ugh. What'd I just say? Not with your mouth full. I'm gonna tell your Grams how you eat when you're here. I know she doesn't let you do that when you're home. Now swallow your food and tell me what was so strange."

He swallowed, and pointed up with his fork. "I happened to look up at the transom window. You know, the small window above the door?"

"Yes, I know what a transom window is. Back when this school didn't have air conditioning, teachers used a long pole to pull it open so the air could circulate. What about it?"

"Well, a big '202' was handwritten in the middle of the glass. Kinda sloppy. Like some workman had marked this transom window for room 202. Of course, that's not the library's room number."

"I don't remember ever seeing that." I took a small bite of my sandwich.

"Right. First time for me, too. But then it got stranger. When I looked again, I watched the 202 just fade away. Last time I checked, the glass was clear."

"Any chance it was a reflection from somewhere in the library, or coming through a window from outside?"

Sonny shoved another ginormous forkful of food into his mouth, and shrugged.

"Did you have one of your gut feelings about it? You know, like it had something to do with a ghost?"

He pushed his glasses up with the same hand that held his fork. "Come to think of it, I don't remember ever just looking up at any transom window before. Not something that would interest me. Maybe I was drawn to look at it?"

"I've been hearing ghosts since I was a little kid," I said. "But you don't. You see ghosts sometimes, but I never see them when I'm by myself."

"Yeah, and I read minds better than you," Sonny said, waving his fork in my direction.

"I agree. And you've even read a ghost's mind. Maybe a ghost is trying to communicate with you."

"Using '202?' " Sonny asked. "What could that mean?"

"You tell me. You're the one who's into decoding."

"How about you go to the library, Bree? See if you see anything on the transom window."

"Let's go together, after school."

Four

Sonny

Fifth period was a loss. All I could think about was the 202 on the transom window. *Why would it disappear? I don't think it's a reflection of anything. If it's a code or a message, who's it from? What's it mean?*

I tried some of the strategies I might use in the Code Breaker game. *The square root of 202 is 14.213. Nothing there. If I squared 202 I get 40804.*

Odd. Both 202 and 40804 are palindromes, because they're the same whether you read them forward or backward. If there's a message in that, I can't figure it out. All I can think of is: 'I'm stuck in the middle.' But that's no help.

Using the telephone pad is another dead end, because the number 2 translates to an A, a B, or a C. But the number 0 has <u>no</u> letter.

Earth calling Sonny! Breanne thought. *Earth calling Sonny!*

Huh? ... Oh, Bree.

Can you turn it down, Sonny? I can't hear Ms Hill over your super intense thoughts.

Sorry. One of the problems with being able to read my mind.

Five

Breanne

Sonny and I are usually the last to leave class because we often get harassed, or bumped, or sometimes punched by the other students. But today I didn't wait to leave last period because I wanted to meet Sonny in the school library. I hustled to my locker, picked up my books, and followed a bunch of kids down the stairs. Sonny was waiting across the hall from the library and looking up at the window above the door. I stopped beside him.

"The glass is clear, like the custodian had just cleaned it," he said. "Let's go inside and look."

A few kids were checking out books when we walked in. I glanced up. The glass was clear on the inside, too.

I whispered. "Where were you when you saw the numbers?"

He pointed with his chin and spoke quietly. "Over there. Science section."

We walked across the room and halfway down the science aisle. Sonny stopped. "Right here."

The shelves are not that high and, being almost all of six-feet tall, I could easily see the transom window. No numbers. But that's no surprise because Sonny's the one who sees spirits, not me. Unless we're touching hands. That's when our powers are magnified, and we can both see *and* hear ghosts.

I looked down at Sonny. At about five-feet two inches he could barely see the transom window over the top of the book shelf. He rose up on tiptoes for a look, then lowered himself to the floor, shaking his head. "I don't see it now."

"You mean you had to get up on your tippy-toes to see the window?"

Sonny nodded.

"I've never seen you walk around on your tippy-toes like a ballerina. What in the world would make you do that?"

"Good question. Guess I felt called to do it."

"What do you mean 'called?' "

Sonny shrugged. "Can't explain it."

"Do you feel any urge to look at the transom window right now, like you did before?"

He shook his head.

"Was the transom window closed when you saw the number, or was it open?"

"Closed."

"So, from this low angle, if the numbers where a reflection, they must have come from high up." I held my hair back and bent down to Sonny's eye level. "I can see a reflection of one of the ceiling lights. But nothing else. Certainly, no numbers."

Sonny rose up on the balls of his feet. "Same here."

Bam!

A heavy book slammed on a desk. We looked back to our left.

"I'm closing up," Mrs. Pidgeon said from across the room. "You two getting any books today?"

"No ma'am," I said. "We'll come back tomorrow."

She watched us walk out. I saw her glance at the transom window.

Did you see that? I thought as we turned down the empty hallway.

I read Sonny's mind. *See what?*

Mrs. Pidgeon was looking at the transom window.

Maybe she saw us checking it out, and just wanted to know what we were looking at.

Maybe...

Six

Breanne

The school library opened every other Saturday during the school year for eighth graders working on their projects. Sometimes the place was full of students. Today when I walked in, I found the library almost empty—just Mrs. Pidgeon, Sonny, and three other students. Sonny was already scribbling away in his notebook at one of the tables, with a stack of books on either side of him.

As I got closer I could read his book titles—mineral deposits, rock formations, asteroids. I dropped my backpack and sat across from him.

"Hey, Bree," he whispered without looking up.

"Hey," I said quietly, as I unzipped my backpack.

He finished writing, closed a book, moved it to the pile on his left, and looked at me, "You gonna work on alternative worlds?"

I nodded, and headed to the book aisles—the one for fiction, not physics. On my way, I noticed one of those really tall wooden stepladders leaning against the wall. I guess the custodian must have been working in here.

I heard a person mumbling—a woman, an older woman I think.

"He's coming, again," the woman said. "Can't do this by myself."

I looked over the top shelf. The remaining students were leaving the library. But they weren't talking. I squatted and peered through the shelves. No one else in the room. *There a ghost in here?* I listened harder. *If the woman is a ghost, I need to hold hands with Sonny so I can see her.*

I went back to the table. Sonny was staring at his notebook. I read his mind. *SOS!*

"What about SOS?" I asked.

"Look!" he whispered, holding a piece of paper. "I wrote '202' on the paper. When I looked on the other side," he said turning the sheet of paper over, " '202' becomes 'SOS,' like in a mirror. It wasn't '202' I saw on the transom window. Someone was writing 'SOS' on the other side of the glass."

I took the paper and held it up. Just like he said, the 'SOS' showed through to the back side.

Sonny pointed at the transom.

I looked up in time to see the number '2' being written on the transom glass. Then we watched a '0.' Then another '2.'

I heard the woman's voice, "He's here!"

Sonny started running. "Help me get this ladder."

I looked around for the woman, but didn't see anyone. I ran after Sonny. We grabbed the ladder and dragged it over to the transom. He pulled on his side and I pulled on my side until we heard the metal locking bars click. Sonny immediately climbed up. I was two steps behind him.

"Bennett?" Sonny said. "Escape from where?"

"Yes, Bennett," the woman said.

"Who's Bennett?" I asked, looking around for the woman.

Sonny pointed. "I think he's on the other side of the glass. Can't see him. Just reading his mind."

"He's my grandson," I heard the woman say. She seemed to be aware of the two of us.

When I reached up and grabbed Sonny's hand I saw her, floating just over Sonny's shoulder—the ghost of an old black woman—in a long cotton dress, wearing her grey hair pulled into a tight bun. She and Sonny were staring at the transom window.

Sonny raised his voice, "I can see you through the glass, Bennett. No! Don't leave!"

"Please don't leave," the woman said, her ghostly hands reaching out.

I couldn't see through the window from my angle. "What's happenin' Sonny?"

"When you grabbed my hand, I saw him. I saw Bennett's ghost," Sonny whispered.

"You saw my grandson's ghost?" the woman asked. "How can you do that?"

Sonny turned. "Who are you?"

"Lorene Turner," the woman said. "Bennett is my teenage grandson."

"But the Bennett I talked to was an old man," Sonny said.

"I know," Mrs. Turner said. "I don't understand it. When I last saw him he was thirteen. I watched him disappear through that transom window."

"You were here?" I asked. "In the library?"

Mrs. Turner looked down at me. "I used to be the librarian here. I was re-shelving some books the day Bennett was sucked through that transom window—twelve years ago. I ran across the room and grabbed his legs. Tried to hold him back, but the pull into the window was too strong. I lost my grip and fell."

Just then I felt a hand grab my ankle. I freaked. "What the...?" I looked down to see Mrs. Pidgeon.

I let go of Sonny's hand. He looked back at me, and saw Mrs. Pidgeon. "We have to get off the ladder," I said.

Sonny took a last look at the transom window. The old wooden ladder creaked and wobbled as we climbed down.

We got caught talking to ghosts, not to mention dragging a ladder across the room and climbing it. *We're in trouble now.* I lowered my head and hid behind my curtain of hair.

Sonny dropped off the last step and bumped into me. "Oops," he muttered.

I kept waiting for Mrs. Pidgeon to go off on us. I peeked through my hair. She was just standing there, her mouth open, looking at us, then up at the transom window.

Mrs. Pidgeon closed her mouth, took a breath. "Come with me," she said quietly.

Is the principal at school today? I thought.

Hope not.

Mrs. Pidgeon stopped at one of the big tables and gestured for us to take a seat. She sat across from us, her hands tightly clasped on the table. When she spoke her voice was soft, her words came slowly. "Is there something special about the transom window?"

Sonny and I looked at one another, then back at Mrs. Pidgeon. "Yes, ma'am," Sonny said quietly.

"I've seen you two looking at the transom before."

We nodded.

"What did you see up there?"

I glanced at Sonny. He was kinda shrinking, looking down at the tabletop. He didn't answer.

"You're not in trouble," Mrs. Pidgeon said. "I have been watching that transom window for years...even before my niece disappeared from this library. So, you can tell me. I heard you say 'Bennett.' Did you see Bennett Turner? Did you see my niece?"

Sonny raised his head, pushed his glasses up. He didn't seem to know what to say.

"Tell her about the '202,'" I said.

Sonny nodded. "I saw the number '202' on the glass last week."

"I've been watching that window all these years, but I've never seen anything, let alone numbers," Mrs. Pidgeon said, glancing up at the transom window. "Do you know what those numbers mean?"

Sonny looked at me. *Do we tell her about seeing ghosts?*

Not sure.

Sonny took a deep breath. "I didn't know last week, but I figured it out today. It's the reverse of 'SOS.' Like in a mirror. When I saw the numbers being written on the glass today I knew someone on the other side was writing 'SOS.' That's why we got the ladder and climbed up."

Mrs. Pidgeon sat back, dropping her hands off the table. "SOS...?" she murmured. Then her eyes got big.

She leaned onto the table, her hands palms down. "So, who was it? Who was calling for help?"

Sonny glanced at me, then back at Mrs. Pidgeon. "Bennett."

"How did you know it was Bennett? You've never seen him. Besides he must be twenty-five by now."

"He told me his name was Bennett. ... And he's a lot older than that."

"Told you? He told you? I never heard anything. And what do you mean 'a lot older than that?' "

Sonny was in trouble. I needed to help. "Mrs. Pidgeon, do you believe in ghosts?"

Her expression changed—from being intense to being scared. She pulled her hands back to the edge of the table. "Why do you ask?"

"Because I don't think we can explain everything unless you do," I said. "So? Do you?"

"Let's say I do believe in ghosts," Mrs. Pidgeon said, her expression returning to normal.

She didn't say no. Sonny thought.

Maybe it'll be okay. Go ahead, tell her.

"You haven't answered my questions, Sonny," Mrs. Pidgeon said.

Sonny looked down. "Well, I didn't exactly see *him*."

"What do you mean, 'exactly'?"

He looked up. "I mean the Bennett I saw wasn't alive."

Seven

Sonny

Tears rolled down Mrs. Pidgeon's cheeks. She pulled a tissue from her sleeve, dabbed her eyes and blew her nose. "Bennett is dead?" she asked softly.

I nodded.

"And you're telling me you talked to his ghost?"

"Yes, ma'am."

She looked around. "I'm so sorry, Lorene."

Breanne grabbed my hand and nodded to the end of the table where the older woman sat, head in her hands, sobbing.

"She's sitting right there," I gestured. "Just above the table. She's crying."

Mrs. Pidgeon's eyes grew wide. "Lorene is there? You can see her?"

I nodded. "When we touch, Breanne and I can both hear and see her."

Mrs. Turner lifted her head. "I raised Bennett after his parents were killed in an auto accident. He was such a good boy." She looked at me. "You saw the same thing I saw, right? The spirit of a very old man."

"Yes, ma'am."

Breanne told Mrs. Pidgeon what Mrs. Turner said, then added, "Say whatever you want to Mrs. Turner, she hears you just fine. I will tell you everything she says back."

"Lorene," Mrs. Pidgeon said. "I'm so sorry about Bennett."

"Thank you," Mrs. Turner said.

"I've missed our long talks, but I felt comforted believing your spirit was here."

"And I have missed being able to talk to you, my dear friend," Mrs. Turner said.

Mrs. Pidgeon looked at Breanne and me. "After forty years as a school librarian, Lorene retired. I became the new librarian. It was my first teaching assignment. I needed a lot of guidance. Lorene was wonderful, coming to the school almost every day to help me learn the ropes."

"You were a fast learner, Marge," Mrs. Turner said.

Mrs. Pidgeon smiled. "Eventually, Lorene told me all about Bennett's disappearance through the transom window, and about how she held on to him for as long as she could before he was sucked into it. I listened, but I didn't believe...not until my niece disappeared."

"You both had relatives at this school?" Breanne asked. "A grandson and a niece?"

Mrs. Pidgeon nodded. "I know, it sounds strange. Even more strange is they were both brilliant children, especially in math and science. We wanted our babies back so much that we watched the transom every school day. We never saw anything. But, one good thing—along the way we became very close."

Mrs. Turner tilted her head and offered a tight-lipped smile.

"Lorene died last year. I have felt her spirit in this library ever since. I knew she would never leave until she knew what had happened to her Bennett. I feel the same way about my niece."

Mrs. Turner spoke up. "Please, young man, tell us everything you heard."

"He told me his name was Bennett and that he was trying to escape from another world."

"Another world?" Mrs. Pidgeon said. "The kids are in another world?"

"He told me he wasn't strong enough to stay at the window because he was being sucked back."

"I can confirm the strength of that suction," Mrs. Turner said. "It is so powerful. It just ripped him from my hands. ... What else did he say?"

"That's all," I said. "He never said anything about being old, or about the other world, or about your niece, Mrs. Pidgeon."

"He say when he'd be back?" Mrs. Turner asked.

I shook my head.

Mrs. Turner rose, floated above the table. "I saw him last week. Watched him write the '202.' I didn't know what it meant. But I saw you looking at it."

"Was that the only other time you've seen him?" I asked.

Mrs. Turner nodded. "I was crushed to see his spirit. To know he had died. And I was shocked to see how much he had aged."

After Breanne told Mrs. Pidgeon what was said, she brought her hands to her mouth. "Oh, Lorene. That must have been so hard for you."

Mrs. Turner lowered to a sitting position above the table. "I tried to go through the transom window to him, but I couldn't get through. I went beside it into the hall, but Bennett was not there. I didn't understand. When I came back around to the window, he had gone."

No one said anything for a long time.

"Listen," Mrs. Pidgeon said, "no one will believe any of this—not the other world, not the transom, and not the ghosts. You can't tell anyone."

"We understand," Breanne said. "Our families know we talk to ghosts, and they're always telling us the same thing."

"I am so grateful the two of you were here," Mrs. Pidgeon said. "I would never have known any of this.

And without you, I would never have been able to talk again with my friend Lorene."

"Yes," Mrs. Turner said. "Thank you, so very much."

"I will be here next Saturday," Mrs. Pidgeon said, glancing to the end of the table. "And I know Lorene will be with me. No other students will be here. Will you come back?"

I nodded. "I'm sure my Grams will be okay with me coming to the library next weekend."

"Same with my Mom," Breanne said.

Eight

Astrobia

The underground complex in the alternate world of Astrobia shook hard. Only hours earlier Leolie had begun her ten-day solitary shift as watch commander at Rynstat, the planet's environmental monitoring station.

She ran to her oversight chamber and stopped dead in her tracks. Brown dust filled the massive wall-sized viewing screen. Debris shot like missiles toward the camera.

"It can't be," she whispered, grabbing at her chest and stepping back, barely able to stand. "All those citizens."

She waved her hand over the console and watched the big screen of real-time satellite videos scroll from one sector of Astrobia to another. Only minutes before, pictures of each area had been filled with dazzling blue dots of life—now in a large section of the country, deadly red dots flashed in their place.

"Whole communities wiped out," she muttered. "Thousands of Astrobians...gone. ... No!"

She zoomed the camera in on Bannar in the southeast quadrant, housing Astrobia's premier scientists—her friends and fellow researchers. Her home.

An expanding mushroom-shaped cloud rose rapidly. The result of the explosion's shockwave was evident in all directions—downed trees, damaged buildings, lifeless bodies.

The door!

Leolie lunged to the control panel at the upper left of the console. She pounded her fist on the gold button, and heard the sucking noise of the protective seals close. Seconds later, the shockwave slammed into Rynstat's above-ground entrance. For the second time that morning, the entire complex shook. She checked the internal air-quality gauge—safe—the seal around the door had held.

She looked up at the screcn. A sea of blinking red lights covered Bannar. "All dead," she gasped.

Leolie called up the list of Bannar scientists and frantically began yelling their names.

"Zardina! Answer me!"

No response.

She called the next name, then the next. No response.

"Anyone! Please!"

No one answered.

She felt her knees weaken and she sank to the floor. Large blue tears—something she had never seen before—splashed off her boot. The sight of those tears awakened her logical brain. Leolie composed herself, hurried to the console.

How bad? Who's left?

She pulled up live power-four level scenes covering the entire country. The big wall screen showed sixteen communities at a time. She scanned the pictures, then waved her hand over the console to move to the next screen of sixteen communities until she had seen all of Astrobia. She looked down at her scribbles—at least eighty percent red lights in three communities, red lights ranging between ten and fifty percent in seven others.

She put out a general call to all first responders. Small pictures of each section commander appeared on the screen as they responded. It took only seconds for the screen to fill up. She recognized General Xigryn's serious face in one of the center frames.

"Situation report!" he ordered.

Leolie took a deep breath before answering. "There has been a massive explosion at Bannar, followed by a powerful shockwave, possibly radioactive. Heavy casualties." She gave the names of the three most affected communities, and then the seven partially affected.

"Understood," Xigryn answered. "All responders, follow Emergency Procedure seven!"

"Leolie, signing off."

She pulled up each of the first three communities, zoomed in, and tried to contact the local leaders.

No response.

She sent out a general call to the community leaders in the seven partially affected communities. The screen changed each time her call was answered, displaying a live video of the individual responding, some were receiving medical attention.

A woman with bandages on her head spoke first. "What in the name of *Qetz the Great* was that?"

"By the shape of the cloud and the force of the shockwave, I'd have to say either a nuclear device or a matter-antimatter collision," Leolie said. "My screen is showing limited signs of life in three communities, and significant casualties in your communities. First responders are in route."

She checked the outside air-quality gauge. "There is mild contamination here at Rynstat. We have to assume the shockwave contained radioactive materials. Use safety precautions. Leolie, signing off."

The wall screen flickered, and Supreme Leader Doric's face replaced everything, his eyes fierce, his voice booming. "Leolie! Report!"

Leolie gave a short bow of her head. "A massive explosion centered at Bannar, Supreme Leader."

"I've tried to contact Zardina. But she did not respond. I have not been able to talk to anyone. Are their communications down?"

"Much worse than that. I fear all at Bannar are dead."

"Dead! All dead? What happened?"

Leolie gave Doric a step-by-step report of the morning's events—what little she actually knew of them.

"No signs of life at Bannar? I can't believe it. I will dispatch my section leaders immediately to get to the bottom of this. And, Leolie..."

"Yes, Supreme Leader."

"As of this moment, you are now my Science Commander, no matter who else may have survived."

Leolie bowed her head, "Yes, Supreme Leader."

"Keeping Astrobia safe must be your only responsibility. I expect a full report in one hour."

His picture disappeared. Flashing red dots returned.

Leolie felt woozy. She staggered to a chair behind the console and collapsed into it. She leaned back, closed her eyes and screamed at the top of her lungs, "Noooo!"

As she opened her eyes, a picture popped into the middle of the wall screen. Nothing but green.

"Identify yourself," Leolie ordered.

No voice.

Only flashes of light and the crackling sound of fire.

The picture changed slightly. More green. Then what appeared to be the edge of a drawing.

Leolie manipulated her console, improved focus, enhanced audio.

Still no voice.

The picture slowly revealed more of the colorful drawing— splashes of blues, reds, bright yellows.

A chakata! A body drawing of a chakata bird. That's Pidge's tattoo!

Leolie tapped her console, freezing the picture of the chakata. "Calling General Xigryn," she snapped.

Xigryn's picture appeared beside the chakata.

General," Leolie said. "I have found a survivor in Bannar."

"I have people at Bannar now."

"Her name is Pidge. She is hurt and there is a fire. She is located on the third level down in Building II, the blue door. There is little time. Her life depends on them."

"Understood," Xigryn said. He signed off, leaving the frozen chakata on the viewing screen.

Leolie tapped her console and the video went live again. Yellow and red flames flickered in the background. "Pidge! Talk to me!"

No response.

"Hold on, Pidge. Help is on the way."

A minute later she heard muffled shouts.

"Here! This way! The blue door!

"Can't get it open."

"Use the blaster."

Boom!

Leolie heard the hiss of carbon dioxide canisters. White smoke filled the picture.

"There she is!"

As the smoke cleared, Leolie could make out white boots and blue protective pant legs—lots of shuffling around. The picture spun—chair and table legs, a shattered window, the blue door lying on the floor.

When the picture stopped moving, she saw a glass-like bubble. A face appeared from behind protective headgear. "We have her, ma'am," the muffled male voice said. "She is alive. Fire is out. Administering aid now."

Nine

Pidge sat at a small grey metal table. Her spiked purple hair stuck out from a white bandage wrapped around her head. A sling cradled her left arm, and a colorful chakata bird tattoo highlighted her light green shoulder.

Leolie set a tray in front of her. "This soup will do wonders for you."

Pidge wrinkled up her nose. "What is in it?"

"A handful of vegetables from our hydroponic garden and just a sprinkle of my special ingredient."

"What special ingredient?"

"Never mind. Just consume it. And do not forget the tea, made from the leaves of the yolish plant. My favorite."

Pidge held out her sling. "I'm left handed."

45

"Well, I am not going to feed you. You are going to have to adapt. Maybe use your feet," Leolie said, smiling.

Pidge made a face and picked up the spoon with her right hand. Only half of the soup made it to her mouth.

Leolie laughed.

Pidge wiped her chin and laughed, too.

"Good start," Leolie said. "Now, be sure to consume every last drop. I have work to do. I will be in the over-sight chamber."

———

Leolie waved her hand over the console as she watched the wall screen, searching for weaknesses in the atmosphere. She made a reference mark on four areas.

The image went black and Doric appeared.

Leolie bowed her head, looked up.

A man stood behind Doric's right shoulder shifting from one foot to the other. A long scar ran along the man's left cheek and jaw bone.

"I have been thinking about your plan," Doric said. "It has suddenly become a possible solution—and an urgent one. Before the explosion we would have had ample time to consider our options. No longer. Tell me again why you believe it will work."

"We lost almost ninety-percent of our scientific community, Supreme Leader. Only thirteen in the science buildings survived the blast."

"And the Science Academy?"

"We have always assumed the large hill that separates the science buildings from the academy would protect the trainers and students from any possible mishap. The theory had never been tested until now. Today the youngest students and their trainers are alive because the lowest floors were protected by the hill. But the top floors of the academy were completely destroyed. Only three trainers and six students from the upper grades are alive. All have significant injuries."

Doric nodded.

"Another twenty-one of us were stationed away from Bannar at the time. Every branch of our sciences has been affected. We are operating with a skeleton crew."

"Yes, yes," he said. "I know all that. But I need to be convinced of the wisdom of your plan to re-open the old portals. We closed them years ago for good reasons. Outsiders got in. They attacked our people and stole our resources."

Leolie nodded. "Zardina created safety features in the old portals. She stopped any passage going out of Astrobia and, to block adult pirates, the portals coming in do not allow any outsider over the age of fifteen to enter."

"Are you certain?"

"Positive, Supreme Leader. Zardina told me herself. When we open the portal, the suction will only flow one way, allowing travel into Astrobia. No being can over-come the suction to travel against the flow, thereby blocking any escape from Astrobia. There is no way any valuables can be taken from Astrobia. The open portals will allow only youth to pass into our world."

"All right. How will you find these teenage beings you talk about?"

"I will refocus the three portals that link to school buildings on alternate worlds. The attraction-proton beams will be programmed to identify the brain patterns of only those young students who are extremely gifted in mathematics, science and problem-solving. The beams will then manipulate their perception centers so the students will be motivated to investigate the portal. As soon as they touch the portal, it will open and they will be sucked inside. Once on Astrobia, our food will modify their brains by adding Astrobian's unique neuro-transmitters, allowing them to learn our scientific ways quickly."

"But we already select students from our own schools and admit them to the Science Academy. Why do we need outsiders?"

"Because it takes years before we benefit from training our own students. Outside students will be different."

"Explain."

"On Astrobia, we are all born with the W-35 enzyme. But no outsiders have that enzyme, and as a result outsiders age rapidly in our world."

Doric glanced back at the man with the scar.

The man nodded. "They grow twenty-years older for every one of our years, Supreme Leader."

Doric again faced the camera. "Go on."

"Consider this example, your eminence," Leolie said. "In only a single year on Astrobia, a thirteen-year old outsider will have physically and mentally matured to thirty-three years of age. During that one year, the outsider's brain will develop at an astounding rate, much faster than our own students' brains."

Doric gestured impatiently. "Continue."

"We feed the outsider advanced neuro-transmitters to develop her brain further. Her brain will demand new information. Our highly sophisticated training program will focus her brain. She will be able to understand complex theories which our students would not be able to understand for another ten years. Just imagine the rapid development of the scientific wisdom and maturity that an outsider, in only a year or two, will quickly be able to contribute to our knowledge base."

"At that rate of aging, she would be over ninety-years old in just four years on Astrobia, if she lives. What do we do then?"

"We capture more replacement students from worlds where we have established a portal entrance."

Doric remained silent for a long time. He stared out from the screen. "Very well, Science Commander. But capture only one outsider to evaluate how well it works. I want regular reports. And make sure you keep the portal closed from our side. I don't want this teenager escaping."

"Yes, your eminence. I will begin immediately."

Doric's face disappeared, and the screen showing the atmosphere returned. Leolie heard a noise and turned to see Pidge standing in the doorway.

"Does he know about me?"

Leolie shook her head. "Now that Zardina is gone, I am the only one who knows."

"Zardina captured me when I was thirteen. I had only been here for two months when she discovered a way to create the W-35 enzyme in the laboratory. By then, I had already aged three Earth years. The enzyme almost immediately turned my skin green and my hair purple. She placed me in the same Science Academy class as you. And now, ten years later, I look like you, I am a scientist like you, and I age like you."

Leolie held Pidge by the shoulders. "We are close friends. And you are one of the smartest scientists on the planet."

Pidge gave a weak smile. "I was Zardina's second capture. Three years earlier she captured Bennett

Turner, another thirteen year old. But back then she did not know how to isolate the enzyme. It was too late for Bennett. I met him only weeks before he died, at the Earthly age of seventy-three."

"You two came through the same Earth portal, right?"

Pidge nodded. "A city called Memphis."

"In that short time, he made a great contribution to our scientific knowledge."

Pidge glanced at the floor, looked up. "Are you going to tell Doric about me?"

Leolie pulled Pidge into a warm hug. "You are like a sister to me, Pidge. I would never tell."

Pidge hugged Leolie tightly with her one good arm. "You are my best friend." She pulled back. "Are you going to re-open that portal to Memphis?"

"It is really the best portal we have," Leolie said. Her eyes grew wide. "You cannot be thinking of going back...of leaving Astrobia? You are not, are you?"

"I miss my grandmother. She is the only family I have."

"I know. But, think about it. First of all, Zardina has altered the portals so no being can escape Astrobia. But even if you could get through the portal, Earth-lings would go wild because your skin would be green. Scientists would put you through all kinds of tests. You would be on display like an animal in a zoo. You would be a prisoner in your own world. You cannot go back."

"I will not be green when I no longer have the W-35 enzyme in me."

Leolie shook her head. "I have no knowledge of how to make the enzyme. Zardina never shared the procedure with me. And the explosion destroyed any hope of finding her notes."

Pidge looked at the floor. "I have always taken a W-35 enzyme injection at the beginning of the cycle of the third Astrobian moon. That was three days ago. My injection was delayed because Zardina was unable to secure the elements necessary to create the special liquid. My body has already been losing the W-35 enzyme. I will stop being an Astrobian within hours."

"But if you stop being an Astrobian, you will be—"

"A two hundred-year old Earthling," Pidge interrupted.

Ten

Sonny

Bree and I said goodbye to Mrs. Pidgeon and Mrs. Turner's ghost. We didn't speak 'till we got outside.

"That was great, Sonny," Breanne said. "You figured out the SOS, got the ladder, and read Bennett's mind."

"Yeah, that was way cool," I said. "Never thought I'd be talking to a ghost on the inside of the transom window."

Breanne looked straight ahead. "It's mind blowing. Who woulda thought there'd be a portal to an alternate world in our library?" She glanced at me. "A physics one."

"How're we gonna get him outta there?"

"Why do ya think Bennett couldn't get through the portal?" she asked.

"I've been wondering about that. He told me he wasn't strong enough to stay at the window. Like he was being sucked back."

"Was he weak because he was the ghost of an old man? Or was the suction super strong. Or, maybe, the portal only goes one way?"

"Or the portal was closed from his side, a way to keep captured kids from coming back to Earth."

Breanne stopped, turned toward me. "Did you hear what Mrs. Turner said about trying to pull Bennett back from the window? It was like once he touched the glass, he was sucked through."

"We're gonna have to be careful," I said. "If Bennett can't put his hands through the glass because his side is closed, we'd have to put our hands through to get him. We could get sucked through."

"It's one thing to reach in and grab a person's hands, then pull like mad and drag him through. It's another thing when that person is a ghost with nothing to grab onto."

"Good point." We started walking again. "You think Mrs. Turner could get hold of him?"

"Don't know," Breanne said. "Can't remember seeing any of our ghost friends grab another ghost, let alone push or pull them. They just kinda go right through each other."

"Gonna have to think about this...a lot."

"I'm not gonna tell my Mom about today, at least not about the portal."

"Agreed. Grams would really flip. What about your grandfather? He always has good ideas for us."

"Maybe. ... Sonny?"

"Yeah?"

"Be real careful. I don't know what I'd do, if you got sucked through that portal."

"Me? What about you?"

"Weren't you listening? Those two kids were really smart in math and science, just like you."

"You thinking the portal's designed to keep everyone out except people who are smart in math?"

Breanne shrugged. "Don't know. But if it is, then maybe it can even attract them. Remember? You said you were 'called' to look at the transom window, something you wouldn't usually do. That's when you saw the '202.'"

"Yeah, but I thought it was Bennett's ghost that got my attention."

"Maybe. ... Did you touch the glass when you were up there?"

I thought back. Pictured Bennett on the other side... "Don't remember. I don't think so."

"For some reason, both of these kids must have touched the glass. Then Bam! There was no way back. Like *Alice in Wonderland*. Nothing happened until she crossed the threshold of the portal, whether it was falling down the rabbit hole or stepping into the mirror. But as soon as she crossed it, she was in an alternate world. Same for the kids who were transported to Narnia through the wardrobe portal."

"Okay. So, what's different? If I'm like them, I shoulda been sucked into the portal too."

"You said Bennett couldn't get through the portal, like it was closed. And Mrs. Turner's ghost couldn't pass inside the transom window. Think the portal's closed in both directions?"

"You saying if it was open I'd've been pulled through?"

"Makes sense."

"So when's it open? And how will we know?

Eleven

Breanne

"See ya Monday," I said, then crossed the street to my house. Sonny raised his hand goodbye without looking at me, and kept walking straight.

This alternate world thing scares me. Who or what is on the other end of that portal? Are they the ones that made Bennett get so old? They wanted him for his intelligence. It's like they drained everything from his body, probably his brain too. ... What about Mrs. Pidgeon's niece? Is she real old, too? What about her brain?

Momma was in the kitchen when I got home. "Get all the books you wanted?" she asked.

I reached back and patted my backpack. "All but one," I said.

"There's cottage cheese and peaches for your snack."

I looked at the round pile of cottage cheese. *Eww.* All I could see was a brain. Bennett's brain. "No thanks. I'm not hungry."

"Suit yourself. It'll be a while 'til dinner."

I dragged myself upstairs to my room. Dropped my backpack, sat at my desk and opened my computer notebook.

Sonny

An honest-to-goodness portal to an alternate world... So cool. What's on the other side? Who's on the other side? Are they friendly? Are they kidnapping people just to study them? Will they be invading earth disguised as Earthlings?

When I stepped inside my house Grams took one look at me and said, "What's wrong? I can see it in your face. Somethin' happened."

Can't tell her about the portal. "Met two ghosts," I said.

"At school? On a Saturday?"

I nodded. "Both pretty old. One a teacher, the other a, er, former student."

"They want you to do somethin'?"

Don't say anything about the alternate world. "They want to be together again."

"Can't they just sit down together and do that?"

"Well, they're kinda in different places."

"Different places? You mean, like one of 'em's trapped?" Grams asked.

"Actually, yes."

"My Grammy told me about this one time a spirit got caught in a different place. Can't remember what she called it. But she had one devil of a time gettin' him outta there. Don't think she was able to do it."

"She work on it in one of her séances?" I asked.

"Can't rightly recall. Like I've told you, back then I was younger than you. All I know is she was always talking to the spirits."

"Sure could use some help on this one, Grams. Let me know if you remember what that 'place' was called."

"Seems like it was a 'p' word."

"Like parallel? Planet?"

"Can't say. I'll have to think on it."

I went up to my room. *My Great, Great Grandmother had tried to help a trapped ghost. The 'p' word could have been portal. What if that ghost was trapped in an alternate world, like Bennett? Did she free it? How'd she do it?*

I googled 'trapped ghosts' online. All I found were a few video games and the super charged trap from the *Ghostbusters* movie. I shifted gears and started scribbling questions.

» How many other portals are there? In Memphis? In the world?

»   Do they all go to the same place?
    To different worlds?
»   Do all worlds have ghosts?
»   Are portals designed to stop ghosts? How do
    they do that?
»   Do portals allow only certain types of people?
    Like really smart ones, or really brave ones,
    or really big or short ones?
»   Can portals be closed and opened?

I stopped writing as questions sprang inside my head like a popcorn machine.

»   *What if I touch the glass?*
»   *Will it suck me inside?*
»   *Where will it take me?*
»   *Who are these beings?*
»   *What do they look like?*
»   *What will they do to me?*
»   *Will they turn me old?*
»   *Will I become an old ghost like Bennett?*

I sat back like I'd just been zapped by a strong bolt of static electricity. Beads of sweat rolled down the lenses of my glasses. I was breathing hard and my pulse was beating rapidly. *I don't want to get sucked into that portal.*

Twelve

Leolie

I picked my way through the ruins at Bannar. I could barely breathe, as if the life had been sucked from me. Everything was covered in a gray ash.

My home... Gone.

No evidence any homes had ever been here. Some science buildings completely leveled. Others with only one wall standing. All plant life turned to ashes in every direction, as far as I could see.

Down the hill behind me, transporter after transporter glided in and zoomed off—loaded with the bodies of my friends and colleagues. People I had gone to school with. People I had worked side by side with. People I had respected—like my dear mentor Zardina. *Such a loss. No one knew as much as she did. No one wiser. Who could possibly replace her as Science Commander? Surely, not me.*

Feeling light-headed, I sat down on a large rock, charred black on the top and one side. I stared unseeing across the barren field. Tears would not stop.

A man's voice broke the silence. "We all share your sorrow," General Xigryn said gently. "My crisis team has been unable to get through even ten-minutes of work without breaking down. The task is immense. The effort is slow. Every second painful."

I looked up, gripped one of his powerful arms.

Xigryn's eyes, too, were filled with tears. He cleared his throat. "You are our Science Commander now, Leolie. I am here for you."

I blinked away more tears. "Thank you."

Pidge

Leolie placed me in charge of the Rynstat monitoring station while she went to see firsthand what the explosion had destroyed. I started on satellite power-four and scrolled through each sector on the wall screen. All appeared well, until I got to the southeast sectors. My heart stopped. Even from this distance the destruction was overwhelming. I searched for any blue lights of life in Bannar. I found only the blue lights of those who were helping. Some of the same people who saved my life...at least for now.

I flipped to zoom power. The three-story Science Academy building is located a few miles from the center of the science complex, on the other side of a small hill. The power of the explosion ripped off the top story and most of the second story. The ground floor, housing the youngest students, appeared untouched. That meant the most advanced students and their teachers on the upper floors didn't make it. It will take years to re-establish the brain pipeline necessary to rebuild the scientific community.

I sat, overwhelmed by all the destruction and loss. Then I considered the prospect of my own demise. *I do not have long before I become part of that brain drain. Without the enzyme, I will stop being an Astrobian. No green skin. No purple hair. No twenty-six year old body. As an Earthling, if I am still on Astrobia, I will begin aging at a furious rate. So quickly that my ghostly body will be joining Bennett before the day is out. I am already three days beyond the beginning of the new cycle of the third Astrobian moon. Three days beyond my scheduled injection. Leolie has to open the portal into Memphis for me, and she has to do it now.*

Thirteen

Breanne

On Sunday I was in my room doing homework when I heard a knock at the front door.

"Bree," Momma called. "Grandpa's here. Wants to see you."

I closed my notebook and hurried downstairs. Grandpa carried a large manila envelope. I knew an old police file was inside. Another 'cold case.'

Grandpa side-hugged me with his free hand. "I've come to see my partner. Well, at least one of my two partners. I have a case and I need help."

Momma shook her head. "I swear, you're just as busy now as you were before you retired from the Memphis Police Department."

Grandpa smiled. "I like trying to crack these old cases that couldn't be solved. Besides, it's fun getting to work with Breanne and Sonny."

"I've got things to do in the kitchen," Momma said. "You two can have your confidential police business discussion in the living room."

Grandpa and I headed into the living room and sat on the couch. He pulled out the police file and opened it to show me a picture of an older Asian man with wire-rimmed glasses. He had a warm smile and was holding a small black dog that looked as if someone had taken a paint brush and painted a white strip from the top of his head, down around his mouth, over his whole chest, and then the insides of his legs.

Grandpa saw me studying the dog. "His dog's a Boston Bulldog named 'Con.' File says that's Vietnamese for 'baby,' pronounced like an ice cream 'cone'."

"Aww. He's so cute. 'Baby' is perfect. Who's the man?"

"This is Nguyen Kim Sanh, regional manager of Winchester Bank & Trust. Apparently, he was never without Con. Even took him to work every day. Bank customers loved to pet him."

"I'd go to that bank."

Grandpa smiled. "Mr. Sanh came to this country as a little boy with his family, after the United States pulled out of the Vietnam War. Back then, Memphis churches and synagogues sponsored a number of Vietnamese families immigrating here. Anyway, Mr. Sanh, like so many of his countrymen, was a hard worker. Over the years he received promotions, all the way to managing one of the regional banks."

"What happened to him?"

"That's just it. We don't know. Mr. Sanh went out for his usual evening stroll with Con and neither one has been seen or heard from since. All we have is a Missing Person Report filed four years ago."

"That's terrible."

"Officers interviewed members of his family and each of the employees at the bank, as well as fellow bank managers who might be competing with him for higher positions in the company. Everyone thought he was a great guy. No enemies."

"So, maybe an accident?"

"If it was an accident, someone worked very hard to cover it up."

"Is Sonny gonna be with us?" I asked. "You know I can't see any ghosts without him."

Grandpa nodded. "I've already talked to him and his grandmother. If you're free now, I'd like to drive you two through the area where Mr. Sanh took his walks in the Central Gardens midtown neighborhood."

"I'm totally free."

Breanne

We picked up Sonny. Both of us sat in the backseat so when the time came, we could touch hands and be able to see any spirits in the area.

After about ten minutes, Grandpa pointed, "This was Mr. Sanh's home. The family no longer lives here. His usual evening walk with Con crisscrossed the neighborhood, never taking the same path two nights in a row. I'll start by driving up and down each of the streets. You kids see what you can see."

We grabbed hands. I watched out the left side, while Sonny took the right. Lots of these homes must be over a hundred years old. We saw ghosts sitting on rooftops, hanging out of windows, and even gliding down the street. But none looked like Mr. Sanh.

"There!" Sonny yelled out. "Beside the big gray house on the corner. That's the ghost of a dog. A Boston Bulldog."

Grandpa stopped the car.

I leaned over. "Is it Con?"

"Can't tell from here," Sonny said. "It's just sitting there, floating above the fire hydrant. Why don't you go out and talk to it, Bree? I'm not goin' out there holding your hand."

I'm sure I rolled my eyes, really big. "You know I won't be able to see it without you. And the only thing I'd be able to hear would be its barks."

"All right, settle down, you two," Grandpa said, looking back at us. "I take it you see a Boston Bulldog?"

Sonny pointed through the open window. We both nodded.

"Let's say it's Con. How 'bout I drive up to her real slow? See if you can get her to jump in the car."

I shrugged. "Okay."

The dog's ghost didn't move as the Grandpa turned the corner, and we got close. Really close.

I nudged Sonny. "Call her name. See if she even looks at us."

Sonny leaned out the window. "Hey, Con."

The dog looked up.

"She knows her name," Sonny said.

"I leaned over beside Sonny, stuck my hand out the window. "Here, girl. Here, Con. Come-on, baby."

"She doing anything?" Grandpa asked.

"She got to her feet and barked," Sonny said. "And she's still looking at us."

"She doesn't know what to think," I said. "I'm sure no living person has talked to her since she became a ghost."

"Keep calling her," Grandpa said, "like you want to play with her."

I tried again. "Come-on, Con. Here, girl."

Sonny joined in. "Hey, Con. Come-on, girl."

"Look," I said, "she's floating this way."

I moved back from Sonny as Con's ghost sliced right through the car door and stopped practically in our laps.

"Now what?" Sonny asked.

"Can't you just pet her?" Grandpa asked.

"No!" we both said.

"Does she have a collar?"

"She does," I said, looking closely. "And it says her name is 'Con.'"

Both Sonny and I jerked back.

"What happened?" Grandpa asked. "She bite you?"

"She's just barking," Sonny said. "Barking a lot."

"I think she's trying to tell us something," I said.

"Maybe the whereabouts of Mr. Sanh?" Grandpa suggested.

I pointed toward the window. "Show us, girl. Show us where your master is."

Con stopped barking and glided out through the closed car door. When she got to the fire hydrant she looked back at us, barked twice, then continued to float away. She disappeared into a small wooded area.

"Let's follow her," I said pushing Sonny.

"I said I'm not—"

I interrupted him. "We don't have to hold hands until we get in the woods. Okay?"

Sonny nodded and opened the back door. We hurried out. I heard a car door close and knew Grandpa was right behind us.

I followed Sonny into the trees and took his hand. As soon as we touched hands, we saw Con coming toward us. She stopped only feet away, barked twice, spun around and disappeared behind a large willow oak tree. We chased her. Just beyond the oak, we found Con hovering above a clearing. The ground beneath her was slightly raised.

We started to walk over when Grandpa put his hands on our shoulders. "Stay here, kids. This looks like a crime scene."

Fourteen

Breanne

Grandpa made a phone call and within minutes lots of police cars pulled up and parked every which way. Then the crime scene team and the coroner arrived. They strung yellow crime scene tape from tree to tree, and began searching the area and taking pictures. Police officers kept everyone back. We were forced so far away so quickly that we never saw them dig up anything.

We sat on the curb, beside the fire hydrant where we first found Con. It looked as if the whole neighborhood turned out to see what was going on. Of course, no one seemed interested in Sonny or me.

I inched my hand over to Sonny's which was on the ground. As soon as we touched pinky fingers I saw Con, lying between us, about a foot off the ground.

She watched the woods, looked back at us every once in a while and whimpered.

Grandpa returned from the woods. "This is gonna take quite a while. Still no sign of Mr. Sanh's ghost?"

Sonny shook his head. "No. Nothing."

I nodded to the side. "Only Con, here."

"And she's pretty worked up," Sonny said.

"How 'bout I take you home?"

"What about Con?" I asked.

"Nothing we can do for her without Mr. Sanh," Grandpa said. "I'm sure she'll be okay here, where she's been for the last four years."

The sun was setting by the time Grandpa dropped off Sonny, then drove me home. I got out, reached into the driver's window, and put my hand on his shoulder.

He put his hand on top of mine. "You were terrific, partner. No one else ever got this far on the Sanh case. I'm confident we'll find the murderer. I'll tell you what the lab uncovers, as soon as I know."

"Yes," I said. "As soon as you know."

Momma met me at the door.

"How'd your detective work go?" she asked.

"We found the ghost of the man's dog. A cute little Boston Bulldog named Con. Con led us to a spot Grandpa said was a shallow grave. He called the Coroner and Crime Scene Team. They were still there when we left."

"A shallow grave. You didn't see any...?

I shook my head. "The police shooed us away. We couldn't see a thing."

"Thank goodness." Momma came over and hugged me. "So, how're you feeling?"

I shrugged. "We left Con there by herself. I'm kinda worried about her."

"You're talking about a ghost of a dog, right?"

I nodded.

"What could happen to her?"

"Nothing, I suppose. Grandpa said she'd be fine. But I'm not sure."

"I think your grandfather is right, sweetie. There's nothing to worry about. Now get ready for dinner."

Sonny

Grams was in the kitchen when I got home. "You get something to eat, child?"

"No, ma'am. I'm starved."

"By the time you wash your hands, I'll have something on the table for you."

I came back downstairs to a feast of fried chicken, collard greens and macaroni 'n cheese. I dug in. Grams sat across from me, drinking her iced tea.

"What's Mr. Thurman got you and your friend doin' that took you so long?"

I took a big bite of the drumstick and started to answer, but Grams held up her hand. I swallowed my food with a painful gulp, then answered. "He was working on a cold case."

"A cold case?"

I nodded. "See, when the police can't solve a case, they put the file and any evidence in a box, then put the box on a shelf. They call them 'cold' cases."

"What was this one about?"

"A man and his dog that's been missing for four years."

"So, he thinks the man's dead, and you can help him because you two can see ghosts?"

"Yes, ma'am."

"Well? You see 'em?"

Not supposed to talk about these cold cases. "We found the dog, but not the man."

"You going back to find him?"

I shoveled another forkful of greens in my mouth, and shrugged.

Grams got up and poured herself more tea. "I been thinking about that ghost you saw at school who was trapped. Been rackin' my brain about my Grammy workin' to save him. Don't think she ever could do it."

I took time to swallow my food, and turned to her. "You mean she wasn't able to free the ghost?"

Grams walked back to the table. "Least ways, that's what I remember."

"Did you remember what that 'p' word was that your Grammy talked about?"

She sat and scooted her chair up to the table. "Near as I recall is that it put me in mind of a hog. Like the ghost was trapped inside a hog."

"A hog?"

"Yup. Think she called it a 'pork,' or maybe a 'porker.'"

"Pork? Any chance she could have been saying 'portal?'"

"Portal? I don't know nothin' 'bout no portal."

Breanne

Next morning, I met up with Sonny for our walk to school.

"Hear from your grandfather?" he asked.

I nodded. "He called last night. Said the Coroner confirmed it was the bodies of Mr. Sanh and Con they pulled out of that grave. Looks like they'd been hit by a car. Found paint stains on Mr. Sanh's clothes. Probably from the car that hit them."

"That'll make a big difference 'cause the police lab has a list of all the paints used on cars going back for more than eighty years."

"Where do you get all this information?"

"I watch more TV than you do."

"Okay," I said. "So, what? Now the police go around checking all the red cars in the city for dents."

"No, silly. They're lots of car companies, and each company uses different shades of paint for their cars. The lab will be able to match the paint found on Mr. Sanh's clothes to the type of car that uses that paint color."

"Huh?"

Sonny gestured with both hands. "Let's say the paint is a shade of red that only Ford uses. Then they'd only have to investigate red Fords."

"Okay. I get it."

We walked on without talking

I said goodbye to Sonny at the second floor, and kept going upstairs to my locker on the third floor to drop off my afternoon books. I'd just closed my locker door when a girl I'd never seen before came up.

"I saw you and your friend Sunday sitting on the curb in Central Gardens, down from where they found the bodies of a man and his dog. Y'all don't even live there."

Can't tell her we were working on a cold case. "My grandfather picked us up from school. He's a retired Memphis policeman. He likes to stay in touch with his old buddies. He often stops when he sees a bunch of police cars. We were just waiting on him."

"That makes sense. But my friend said it was because you two had done something to that poor man and his dog. You know, used your witchcraft on them. Made them disappear."

"We did no such thing," I said, raising my voice. "What in the world are you talking about? Where'd you get such a crazy idea?"

"That's what Deena told everyone. Said you used witchcraft on her."

"Really? You believe Deena? Don't-cha know she was just expelled from school for bullying and stealing from a teacher? How could you trust anything she'd say?"

The girl thought for a second. "So she just made up the witchcraft stuff?"

"Of course. If I were a witch I'd make up a potion so I'd be the most popular kid in school."

She nodded and smiled. "Yeah. Right. You'd really need a lot of potion to do that." She turned and walked away.

"Please tell your friend I'm not a witch," I said to her back.

She raised a hand.

That was weird. First, I'm worried about some-one knowing we were sitting with a ghost dog. Then, I'm worried about Deena telling everyone I'm a witch because our ghost friends did things to her she couldn't explain. And finally, I get slammed by a kid I've never even seen before who tells me there's not enough potion in the world to keep me from being a total loser.

Fifteen

Leolie

The outer Rynstat door slid open with a whoosh when I passed by the sensor. I found Pidge in the oversight chamber.

Pidge looked straight ahead. "Just watched you at Bannar." She paused. "Is it as horrible there as it appears on the screen?"

"Worse," I said taking a seat beside her. "I could feel the souls of all our people. I could hear their cries."

Pidge found my hand and gently squeezed.

I squeezed back. We stayed that way for a long time—two friends, both grieving our loss, both emotionally exhausted.

Pidge broke the silence. "My remaining hours in this world are few. ... I have no choice but to try to get back to earth through the portal."

"Doric has agreed for me to open the portal coming from earth long enough to capture one teenage outsider. But he has forbidden me to open that portal from our side. He does not want anyone leaving Astrobia."

Pidge turned to me. "Please, Leolie. My body will soon use up its remaining store of the enzyme, and the only supply was destroyed in the explosion. I am already losing my strength. And without the enzyme, I will age instantly here on Astrobia. I am not even sure my changing body would survive a trip through the portal. But getting back to earth is my only hope."

I nodded. "Okay. … But we must plan this carefully—for your safety and for mine. I admit Doric scares me. I don't know what he would do if he learns of this."

"Thank you," Pidge said, squeezing my shoulder.

I drew strength from her, then pulled back and took a deep breath. "First, we need to determine how many hours you have left. When will the enzyme be completely gone from your system?"

"I don't know. I have not experienced being in such a state. I was to have my injection three days ago. That would have allowed me to maintain an even level of the enzyme."

"There must have been times when your monthly injections were late. What happened then?"

Pidge nodded. "Over the years my injections were delayed a few times because Zardina had been unable to create enough of the enzyme, but never more than two days. I remember feeling weak on the second day, and the green in my skin started to fade." She held out her arm to show the change in color. "Like now."

"Would you say the enzyme would have completely left your body by the third day?"

Pidge did not answer right away. "As quickly as my body is changing, I believe most of my Astrobian physical characteristics will be gone by day's end. No longer than tomorrow."

"That's it then," I said. "We must plan for your return. It would be best if we could time your leaving as close as possible to the outsider's arrival. That would keep others from being able to detect the opening of the portal leading away from Astrobia."

Pidge took a deep breath and exhaled loudly.

"Instruments have recently detected a candidate with the intellectual capacity we need—a male, I believe. I have already opened earth's side of the portal. But I cannot predict when he will be near enough for our sensor beam to lure him into the portal."

Pidge shook her head. "My leaving through the portal would cause a disruption of the electro-magnetic monitor."

"Yes, but the disruption caused by an alien coming to Astrobia through the portal might be enough to cover the disruption of your leaving."

"But there is no way to predict when an alien would be coming through the portal. And without that diversion, Doric's people would know you opened the portal leaving Astrobia. You'd be caught disobeying an order. I cannot let you take that risk."

"And I cannot let you stay," I said. "I cannot bear the thought of watching you grow old right in front of me."

"What do we do?"

"We need a plan."

Sixteen

Sonny

Saturday morning, Breanne and I left for the school library. Mrs. Pidgeon stood when I opened the library door. She clearly was not expecting any other students. She wore old jeans, tennis shoes and a University of Memphis sweatshirt. The custodian's super big step-ladder spread open across the doorway. Bree and I had to duck under it to get into the room, banging our backpacks against the side rails.

Even before I cleared the ladder, Mrs. Pidgeon began talking without taking a breath, like someone had let the air out of a big balloon. "Thank you so much for coming. As you can see, I arranged to have the ladder just in case. And I'm certain Lorene is here too. Would you check?"

We shrugged out of our backpacks and Bree took my hand. We found Mrs. Turner floating just above the ladder, looking through the transom window.

Bree pointed with her chin. "There she is. Up there."

"Morning, children," Mrs. Turner said, keeping her eyes on the glass.

"Good morning," we said in unison.

"I knew you were here, Lorene," Mrs. Pidgeon said, looking up. "So, what do we do now?"

"I have not left this transom window since last Saturday," Mrs. Turner said. "There has been no sign of Bennett."

Mrs. Pidgeon looked at Breanne.

Bree repeated Mrs. Turner's words.

Mrs. Pidgeon looked at the transom. "Have you tried to go through the portal, Lorene?"

"Only a thousand times," Mrs. Turner said. "But I cannot get through."

"I think we just have to wait," I said. "Mrs. Turner will be watching. She'll let us know if anything happens."

Breanne let go of my hand and walked toward the rows of books. "There're one or two books I have to find. Don't worry, I'll be able to hear Mrs. Turner if Bennett shows up."

"Okay," Mrs. Pidgeon said, "as long as you can hear Lorene. I have books that need to be put on the shelves."

I followed Breanne. She turned at the fiction aisle. I went down the science and physics aisle. I pulled a book and began looking for anything on parallel universes or alternate worlds. The oddest thing happened. I thought I felt a draft. Like a window opened and cool air rushed in. I checked, but none of the windows were open. I looked at Bree and Mrs. Pidgeon. Neither seemed to notice.

Then, like before, I was drawn to look at the transom. Without taking my eyes off the transom, I closed the book and shoved it back on the shelf. I can't explain it, but my feet just started taking me to the ladder. In the distant background I barely heard Breanne.

"Mrs. Turner says Bennett's coming," Breanne said. "Sonny. Where're you going? Sonny?"

I looked down. I was climbing the ladder, only two more steps to the top.

I faintly heard Breanne. "Sonny! Answer me! What are you doing?"

Breanne grabbed my ankle. I could see Mrs. Turner's ghost pointing at the transom window. I felt someone grab my other ankle. Even though I didn't see her, I knew it was Mrs. Pidgeon. Then I was at the top step, staring into the transom window. I saw Bennett's hands on the other side of the window. I reached out and touched the glass. My hand disappeared. I reached after it with my other hand. It disappeared. I couldn't believe the pull. I was being sucked into the portal.

My face broke through the surface. "Hey!" I yelled into the emptiness. "Get me outta here!"

I couldn't hear my words. No echo. It was like yelling against a super big pillow. The portal just swallowed my voice.

Bree still had my ankle, so I was able to catch a glimpse of Bennett's ghost rapidly moving away from me.

My arms flailed around inside the portal. I had nothing to grab onto, like I was leaning over the edge of Grand Canyon. I bent at the waist and pressed my thighs against the top of the door to keep from going all the way through the glass, but the suction was too strong.

I was losing the tug of war, being pulled further into the portal. Now up to my waist. My thighs started sliding over the edge. Within seconds I was lifted over the edge. I felt Breanne's and Mrs. Pidgeon's weight, like they were swinging in the air. Then it happened.

First Mrs. Pidgeon, then Breanne, lost their grip on my ankles. I fell completely into the portal, instantly speeding up like a jet taking off from an aircraft carrier. Everything blurred as I blasted through a time-space continuum—from one planet to another. I couldn't breathe. The pressures were unbearable, whipping my arms every which way, trying to yank them out of their sockets. My body spun and tumbled. I finally pulled my arms in and locked them across my chest.

Just when I thought I'd completely run out of breath, I began to slow down. A light appeared ahead. I dropped feet first. I imagined I was parachuting into a large room. My legs crumpled when I hit the floor so hard my teeth clamped together. If my tongue had been hanging out I would have cut it clean off. I ended in a heap. My glasses flew off, and I heard them scrape across the floor.

I stayed there for a while, catching my breath. Everything was spinning, and I felt sick to my stomach. I held my head straight. When the spinning stopped, I began moving my arms, then my legs. My shoulders hurt. But no broken bones.

I raised my head, but nothing was in focus. I started feeling around on the floor for my glasses. My hands hit something—I could make out boots. Boots with green legs. I followed the legs up. Brown shorts.

"You looking for these?" a female voice asked, holding out my glasses.

I took my glasses, fumbled them on. I snapped back.

A green woman! Purple hair!

Instead of white around her big brown eyes, the sclera were bright yellow. She was slender and muscular. About my height. And there was a brightly colored drawing on her shoulder.

"I'm Pidge," she said, looking down at me. "And you are...?"

"Sonny," I squeaked. "Sonny Etherly."

She held out her green hand.

I jerked away.

"Don't be afraid," she said, reaching her hand closer.

I didn't move.

"Come on. It is okay."

My hand moved slowly to hers. She grabbed it and pulled me right up like I was a bag of feathers. Once on my feet I could see she was just a bit taller than me, but way taller if you counted the spiky purple hair.

Then it dawned on me. "Pidge? ... Like Pidgeon? Like Mrs. Pidgeon in the school library."

Her eyes widened. "My aunt Marge? On Earth? You know her?"

"I was just talking to her when...when I was sucked through the transom window. She's been looking for you, all these years."

Pidge turned serious. "And I so want to be with her, as well."

"But you're green. And you're supposed to be a teen-ager. And you've got a ... a tattoo."

"I look like every other Astrobian female, except no one else has a tattoo of a chakata bird."

"That's a bird?"

Pidge nodded. "Every being on Astrobia knows the brilliantly colored chakata bird. It is very rare, and it brings good fortune just to see one."

"Astrobia? Where...? Where are we? Where's Earth?"

"We are on the planet Astrobia in a parallel universe, only five hundred million light years from the universe that's home to Earth."

"Five-hundred million... How'd I get here so fast?"

"Going through the portal is kinda like travelling through hyperspace," a man's voice said.

I turned, but no one was there. *Did I hear a man speaking? Or did I read someone's mind? ... Could it be? ...* "Bennett?" I asked. "Is that you?"

It is indeed, Bennett thought. *I could not fight it. Got sucked back to Astrobia when you were pulled through the portal."*

"You <u>and</u> your grandmother?"

No. Just me. I truly wanted to be with you both, but on the <u>other</u> side of the portal.

Pidge looked around, then back at me. "Who are you talking to? ... You said, Bennett. The only Bennett I know is Bennett Turner. But it can't be that Bennett. He's dead."

I looked down. "Sometimes I can read minds..." I looked up. "Even the minds of ghosts."

"Ghosts?"

"I met Bennett's ghost and his grandmother's ghost last week at the transom window."

"The transom? Bennett's ghost was trying to get back to earth? What's this about his grandmother?"

"Like your aunt, his grandmother has been waiting for him to return. She passed last year, and now her ghost waits for Bennett. From what he said, he was dragged back here today by the same force that brought me."

Pidge looked around again. "Where is he now?"

I shrugged. "I can't see him. Can't hear him either. Only read his mind."

Tell her I'm standing beside you, on your right.

I nodded to my right. "Bennett says he's standing next to me."

Pidge took a half-step back, then slowly raised her hand, chest high. "Hello, Bennett."

Hello, Pidge.

Seventeen

Breanne

Sonny yelled and squirmed as the portal gradually pulled him inside. I tightened my grip on his ankle with both hands and was lifted right off the ladder.

Even though his head was inside the portal, I was able to read Sonny's mind. *Help me! I can't stop it. Pull harder!*

His body jerked farther inside. I swung in the air, my feet waving around, searching for something to stand on.

I felt Sonny's sock begin to slide down. I squeezed tighter, but no matter how hard I tried, I couldn't hold on any longer. I fell backwards.

My concentration was so intense that I saw everything in slow motion. Just beyond my outstretched fingers, I watched Sonny's white socks and black hard-soled shoes disappear inch-by-inch through the transom window.

Then my butt hit the floor hard. Jarred me all the way up my spine, and I bit my lip.

I must've sat there motionless for two or three seconds, stunned. When I came to, my fingers bumped into my glasses that had fallen into my lap. I put them on, looked up that tall ladder, and saw the overhead light reflected off the transom window. Then everything came rushing back to me.

"Nooo!!! Sonny!"

What just happened? I can't believe it. How could he be gone? Through a transom window? It's all my fault. I let him go. He's not coming back.

Tears filled my eyes. *Sonny's gone!*

"Breanne!" Mrs. Turner said. "Quick. Marge needs help."

Huh?

"Hurry!"

Mrs. Turner?

I heard moaning and caught movement to my left. So hard to see through my tears. I pulled off my glasses and blotted my eyes with my sleeve. When I put them back on I saw Mrs. Pidgeon lying on the floor on the other side of the ladder—moaning, squirming. I quickly crawled to her on my hands and knees.

All color had drained from her face. Mrs. Pidgeon clutched her chest with both hands and couldn't seem to catch her breath. Her hand shot out, reaching toward her desk.

"Pills!" Mrs. Turner said. "In her purse!"

I ran to the teacher's desk and yanked open drawers 'till I found Mrs. Pidgeon's purse, then hurried back to her. *Please don't die.*

She raised her head and snatched the purse, but couldn't find the little puller-thing on the zipper. She cried out in pain, clutched the purse to her chest, and dropped her head back to the floor.

I yanked the purse from her hands and quickly unzipped it.

"Pill box," she hissed through her clenched jaw. "Green."

I dug through her purse and found a small bright green plastic container. I snatched it, popped it open and held it in front of her. She jabbed her fingers into it, knocking most of the small, round, white pills to the floor.

When I looked up, she had one pill between her finger and thumb. She stuck it under her tongue, closed her mouth, and gripped my forearm.

Mrs. Pidgeon kept one hand on her chest the other holding my arm so tight I lost feeling in my fingers. We stayed like that for what seemed like forever, but it was probably only a minute, maybe two. Finally, her grip relaxed, and I heard her breathe more calmly.

"You're a Godsend, my dear," Mrs. Pidgeon said softly. "Bad heart. Nitroglycerin pills are a miracle."

I stood. "Let me help you up."

She shook her head. "Makes me dizzy. ... Need to stay here for a while. ... But I'll be fine now."

"Get a mattress from the nurse's office," Mrs. Turner said. "Marge has the key on her keychain, in case any students need medical help."

I dug through the purse till I heard them jingle. I held them up. "Which key unlocks the nurse's office?"

Mrs. Pidgeon pointed. "The one with the white tape on it."

I ran down the hall to the nurse's office and unlocked the door. I found two thin mattresses, grabbed them both and a pillow, then dragged them back.

I helped Mrs. Pidgeon slowly roll on top of the mattresses. I held her head up and slipped the pillow underneath.

"Thank you, dear," Mrs. Pidgeon said. "That's so much better."

I took a deep breath, feeling so relieved. I felt my shoulders relax.

That's when it hit me—*Sonny!* I remembered that Mrs. Pidgeon had been holding Sonny's other ankle. She must have fallen, too. The strain must've caused her heart attack. *Sonny.*

I dropped to one knee and began crying again.

Mrs. Pidgeon reached over and held my hand.

Eighteen

Sonny

An Astrobian woman came into the room talking. "I just saw the electro-magnetic readouts from the portal. We have a—"

"A new teenager from earth," Pidge said, finishing her sentence. "Meet Sonny. Sonny, this is Leolie, our Science Commander."

Although the same size and build, Leolie was much more colorful than Pidge—her skin an iridescent green, hair deep purple, and flashing brown eyes surrounded by bright yellow. She looked me over and cocked her head. "Did you also have black skin and brown eyes, Pidge?" she asked.

Pidge waved her hand. "No. My skin was more cream colored and my eyes were hazel. Unlike Astrobia, we Earthlings do not have just one skin color or one eye color. Our skin could be some shade of brown, black, pink, yellow or red. And our eyes could be some shade of brown, blue, gold, green, or a blend we call hazel."

"Interesting," Leolie said. She turned to me, "Welcome to Astrobia, Sonny."

"I'm not supposed to be here," I said. "I got sucked through a window."

Leolie gave a half-smile and led Pidge away. I couldn't make out what they were saying.

They are talking about opening the portal to let Pidge go back to Memphis, Bennett thought. *If they do that, I will be able to tag along.*

"I'm going with you," I whispered.

Don't know how. Leolie wants to lock you up so you can't get away.

"Lock me up?" I whispered. *Moon rocks! I'll end up just like you.*

Pidge started to collapse. Leolie caught her, and pulled her to a chair.

"Now what?" I whispered.

Can't explain everything right now. But Pidge is growing weaker by the minute...it won't be long before she will begin aging.

"Like you did?"

Oh, much faster than I did. She has to get out of Astrobia today. This planet makes us Earthlings age very rapidly.

"How rapidly?"

About twenty earth years for every one Astrobian year.

"What? That's twenty days for each day here."

Actually, it's twenty-point-zero-three days.

"What are you? Some kind of math whiz?"

Yes. Just like you, only a bit more experienced. That's why the Astrobians captured us—for our mathematical brains.

I heard the sound of boots and turned to find Leolie right up on me—nose to nose. She grabbed my upper arm in a vise grip.

"Come with me."

I had no choice. She walked as fast as Breanne, even though she was more my size. When she passed in front of a sensor the door slid open with a quiet whoosh. She pulled me into a room that looked like a sterile medical clinic—gray metal walls, no windows, one metal table and one metal chair the only furniture. She sat me down.

"You will stay here," she said, then spun around and walked out.

"Wait," I said. "How long?"

Leolie talked over her shoulder. "Until I say different."

The door whooshed shut.

Until I say different. My mouth went as dry as Death Valley. I felt my stomach drop to my ankles. Panic set in. *I'm doomed if I can't get outta here. And even if I can get outta here, where do I go? Bennett never got away. Pidge is still here. I'm sure they're smarter than me.*

Nineteen

Bennett

I floated behind Sonny as Leolie marched him into the chamber. He looked so scared, so hopeless—shoulders collapsed, staring into space. He reminded me of how I felt the day I was captured and locked in the very same chamber. I thought I would never get back to earth.

This is my last chance. If Leolie opens the portal for Pidge, I can go with her.

Sonny sat up. "Hey! I heard that, Bennett. What about me? You have to take me with you."

I forgot Sonny could read my mind. If I were alive my face would be beet red with embarrassment. *So sorry. But really, Sonny, I don't see any way I can help you do that.*

"I do! Start by finding out Leolie's plan. What's she gonna do and when's she gonna do it?"

Yes, of course. I can do that. Be back as soon as I know something.

I zoomed through the walls and found Leolie entering the eating chamber. Pidge was sitting in a chair, bent forward, her elbows on her knees. Tiny blotches of faded green areas appeared on her skin, and her purple hair was not as bright as it had been. Signs of her deteriorating health. *Not good signs. Not good at all.*

Leolie lowered to one knee beside Pidge and placed a hand on her shoulder. "How are you feeling?"

"Not great. ... Got weak for a minute. ... Thought I was going to pass out. Still feel a bit odd."

Leolie stood. "The W-35 enzyme must be leaving your body faster than you thought. That means you will be changing from an Astrobian back to an Earthling very soon."

Pidge looked up. "Back to a really <u>old</u> Earthling. And then..." She took Leolie's hand. "I don't have much time. Please, I must leave Astrobia. Open this side of the portal. Let me go back to earth, no matter what condition I will be in."

Leolie did not answer for a long time. "Okay. I will do it. But I have to be careful. I know Doric has his people searching for any indication that the portals are being used. In fact, I expected him to have contacted me by now about Sonny's arrival."

"You think they weren't able to detect the changes in the electro-magnetic field as he entered Astrobia?"

Leolie shrugged. "The changes are slight and don't last long. That makes them hard to discover if you are not specifically looking for them at the exact time they occur."

"Then, Doric doesn't know Sonny's here?"

"So it appears. I guess we are safe for the moment."

"Will he know when the portal is open to leave Astrobia?"

Leolie looked down, as if thinking. "No. Not when it is open. But he could discover you going through the portal."

"We need a diversion. Something that takes their attention away from the portal, just for a few seconds."

Leolie nodded. "Doric is expecting my report on the cause of the explosion. I will not have time to work on the portal until after I finish my investigation. I need to be gone for a while. Can you handle the observation room while I'm out?"

"I think so."

Leolie walked Pidge to the observation chamber, then left.

Twenty

Sonny

I pounded on the door. "HELP! GET ME OUTTA HERE!"

I'll be like Bennett in no time. I'm freaking out.

Bree? Can you read my mind? Bree?

Nothing.

What would Grams say? She'd tell me I have to man-up, like my Marine daddy in Afghanistan does every day. He always does his job, no matter who's shooting at him or trying to blow him up. No matter how scared he might be.

I can hear her now, 'You can't just mope around, child. You're smart. Now use that brain of yours and your special senses.'

And she'd remind me how many problems Breanne and I have figured out when we worked together.

But how can I do that? Breanne's in another world and I have no way of contacting her.

Contact her? Is there a way?

Twenty-One

Bennett

I zipped back to Sonny's room and found him pacing from one side to the other. He looked up.

He can see me. I thought.

Sonny shook his head. "Can't see you, but I can sense your presence and read your mind. What's goin' on?"

Pidge is not well. Her body is losing the Astrobian W-35 enzyme that keeps her from aging. I do not think she will see tomorrow. She wants to return to earth before she dies. Leolie agreed to open the portal for her even though Supreme Leader Doric has ordered that all portals remain closed. Pidge does not want Leolie to get into trouble. She said they need a diversion to keep anyone from seeing the change in the electro-magnetic field when she passes through the portal. But Leolie has left Rynstat to investigate the explosion and report to the Doric. They will develop a plan later.

Sonny sat in the metal chair and appeared to be in deep thought.

I couldn't hide my honest thoughts any longer. *I'm sorry, Sonny. There's nothing we can do.*

Sonny looked in my direction. "We need to help Leolie in her investigation, so she'll be free to work on the portal."

Help Leolie? How?

"First tell me about this explosion."

Very bad. Thousands of Astrobians lost their lives, mostly scientists.

"Scientists?"

Yes. It happened in an area of Astrobia called Bannar where almost all scientists and their families lived and worked.

"I don't get it. Why're all the scientists living together?"

It goes back to before I was sucked through the portal. Before I was captured. ... There are lots of volcanoes on earth, right?

Sonny nodded.

Same on Astrobia. About fifteen-years ago, five or six of them erupted, one right after the other. A few really big ones near population centers. It would be like the monster earth volcanoes at Krakatoa and the Yellowstone Supervolcano blowing at the same time.

"That would be huge. They reshaped the earth and killed lots of people."

Precisely. To make things worse, Astrobia is a much smaller planet than earth. Almost half of the population was killed.

"Holy moon rocks."

From what I have learned, it was a chaotic time. Citizens were terrified. The Supreme Leader was blamed for not protecting the people. There were even protests and riots. A very strong, aggressive military general took over as Supreme Leader.

"Let me guess—Doric."

That's right. Commanding General Doric named himself Supreme Leader and mandated a new program to develop scientists to monitor the volcanoes and keep the planet safe. Scientists were elevated to high positions of authority. They opened a Science Academy to train students and built several high-tech science buildings—all located in Bannar, the furthest point from any volcano.

"So this recent explosion was another volcano?"

I do not think so. Looks more like the anti-matter generator at Bannar.

"Anti-matter? You have an anti-matter generator?"

Had six for the whole planet. Now there are five.

"This is what Leolie's investigating?"

Yes. Doric ordered her to find out what happened.

"She have any ideas?"

Said it might have been an accident, or it might have been done on purpose to get rid of the scientists.

"Who'd want to get rid of scientists?"

After the volcanoes erupted, a lot of leaders were demoted. Made them angry. Could have been one of them.

I thought for a second. "Okay. ... Tell me what you are capable of doing."

Huh?

"As a ghost. You know. Like back on Earth, ghosts seem to be stuck in one place. They stay in the same house or the same school unless they get attached to an object that gets moved to another building. Can you travel outside this building?"

Travel? Well, yes. Bannar was my home—where I lived and worked. ... And where I died. But I've never had any problems leaving my home or going from place to place.

"What about moving things. Some Earth ghosts I've met can move physical things—pick things up, throw things, push buttons. But other ghosts can't."

Zardina was the Science Commander when I got here. Even though she is the one who captured me, she had always been good to me. After I died, I spent a lot of time hanging around her lab. She never knew I was there. Zardina had gotten pretty old, even for an Astrobian. Been getting forgetful lately. I would help her with little things, like put lids back on bottles, pick up after

her, and move her glasses close to her when she could
not seem to find them.

"Perfect. I think we can work together."

Work together? On what?

"I have a friend named Breanne. When we touch
hands, we both can see and hear ghosts. Her grandfather is a retired policeman. Sometimes he asks us
to help him investigate crimes. I think you and I can
investigate this explosion."

Okay...?

"First we need facts from the scene. You've spent a
lot of time in the labs. You'd know if something looked
different, even suspicious, right?"

Yes, I think I would.

"Go to Bannar. Check around. See what you can
find."

I can do that. What are you going to do?

Well, the police are always reviewing security cameras to see if there's a shot of the criminal. I need to
look at the videos of Bannar."

Pretty sure the explosion obliterated any monitoring
recordings in the area.

"I was thinking about the video footage here? There
must be a way to review it."

Of course. But how are you going to see it?

Sonny pointed. "There's a video screen hanging on
the wall right there. Do I need a keyboard or does it
take verbal commands?"

You can use either one. For verbal, just begin each command with the name: 'Ellie.'

"I'm sure there's a way to stream the information from the observation chamber to this screen. Can you take care of that?"

Let me see what I can do.

Twenty-Two

Bennett

I floated through the wall, into the observation chamber and stopped. It was surreal—an enormous picture filled the wall screen of what used to be the living quarters in Bannar. Pidge, standing in front, made it look as if the picture was three dimensional. I was horrified. Bannar was...gone.

The image reminded me of old pictures I had seen from the end of World War II, after the atomic bomb destroyed the Japanese city of Hiroshima. The only things left standing were busted shells of the buildings. No trees. No statues. Debris covered the ground.

A handful of green skinned people were picking their way through the rubble. One of them was Leolie. Every once in a while she would squat and pick up an object, look at it, then let it fall back to the ground.

I drifted over the console and pressed the button that streamed the camera into Sonny's chamber. Then went back to check on him. He had already begun trying out commands.

"I've got this," Sonny said, watching the screen images roll by. "You check the science buildings at Bannar. Maybe you can find something Leolie needs for her investigation."

I spun around and zoomed through the chamber wall, then up through the dirt covering the station's ceiling, and out to Bannar. *All these years I have never seen an Astrobian ghost. Do not know if that means there are no ghosts, or I am on a different spirit plane. I wonder if I will see some today.*

I had my answer when I arrived—not a single ghost. The scene was exactly as I had just seen it on the wall screen. Astrobians sifted through the rubble. I could see by their uniforms they were from the military. Leolie gave them instructions on things to look for that might help her determine what caused the explosion.

Two partial walls stood just beyond them, the only evidence that three science buildings had ever existed. The battered walls were a dusty cement color with black soot covering the inside.

I passed over Leolie and dove down to Zardina's lab on the third underground level in what used to be the main building.

The lab's low intensity safety lights were powered by prized elements, that on my home planet are called 'rare earths.' Even the explosion didn't knock out those lights. A soft red glow covered the entire lab. I drifted over to Zardina's desk. She would probably have been here at the time of the explosion. But there was no sign of her. Her body must have been collected by the emergency crew.

Unlike the above-ground floors, the lab had not been demolished. But the explosion's concussive force had created large cracks in the walls and floor. Nothing but dust remained on the lab tables, desks and shelves. Pieces of broken glass covered the floor. Each piece reflected the red light creating an eerie scene, as if the floor were on fire.

I focused on Sonny's request—anything out of the ordinary. Anything that would provide a clue as to what happened.

Nothing.

I slipped into the storage bay, down the hall. Bins of prized elements used in the production of cutting edge technology sat row after row. These elements reduced the weight of high-tech devices and increased their power as well as battery life.

A heavy metal door covered the front of each bin. None was open. Yet minute pieces of silvery elements and their silver dust lie all around. I never saw the bay look like this. It was as if someone had carelessly taken the prized elements from the bins and scattered them the way a farmer casts seeds.

I heard footsteps. The door opened and Leolie entered. She swept the room with her high intensity flash light and stopped on the exact spot I had been studying. She came closer, reached down, brushed the silver dust with her fingers, and inspected it. She then shook each bin cover to make sure they were secure.

I followed Leolie as she checked every other room in the complex. Inside Zardina's lab she collected as much as she could of her obliterated computer, dropping the pieces into a shoulder bag. I didn't see her collect anything else that would give us a clue as to what had happened.

Leolie tapped her belt. "Pidge."

"Pidge here."

"I'm returning to Rynstat."

"Understood."

"Leolie signing off." She tapped her belt again.

I decided to hitch a ride in her two-seat transporter, with the cockpit seats set up like our jets on Earth. I sliced through the side and stretched out in the back seat just as she lifted off. When we arrived at Rynstat I floated in beside her.

Leolie went straight to the observation chamber. Pidge sat behind the console. "How are you, Pidge?"

Pidge sat up straight. "I am hanging on. ... I watched you on the screen. It must have been awful."

Leolie lowered her head. "Yes. Awful."

Pidge waited before she asked, "You learn anything?"

"Particles of prized elements were on the floor in the storage bay."

"From the explosion?"

Leolie shook her head. "Do not think so. The bin covers were all closed and latched. Even the concussive blast hadn't opened them."

"That floor is always kept spotless. Every particle can be used."

"Right. So why were they on the floor?"

"Someone stealing them?" Pidge asked.

"That is what I am thinking."

"Anything else?"

"I checked Zardina's lab. Picked up pieces of her computer. The bank of computer servers above ground on the second floor was completely wiped out. No way to recover decades of general scientific data, let alone Zardina's work." Leolie patted her shoulder bag. "I am not hopeful, but I will see if I can read anything from her computer."

"Like the W-5 enzyme formula?"

Leolie nodded. "I will work on it. You study the high-powered view of Bannar before the explosion."

"What am I looking for?"

"Anyone who doesn't belong," Leolie said as she walked away.

Pidge backed up the video to the morning of the explosion, and zoomed in. Instead of blue flashing lights seen at the lower power setting, she clearly saw lines of transporters converging on the science buildings and the school to empty their passengers. The youth had maroon hair, while the young adults' hair was bright purple. The purple began to dull in the older Astrobians, with the oldest citizens having an almost brown hair color.

Pidge's eyes filled with tears as she recognized friends. She continued to watch until the explosion overwhelmed the screen with rocketing debris, followed by clouds of smoke and dust.

Twenty-Three

Sonny

"Ellie!" I said. "Standard power."

"It is not necessary to raise your voice," Ellie announced matter-of-factly in a young woman's calm voice. "My sensors are sufficient to process your commands, even when given within the decibel range of a whisper."

"Sorry," I said. "I didn't mean to yell at you."

"No need to apologize," Ellie said. "I am never offended. I also understand seven distinctive English accents. I believe yours will make eight."

I'm having a conversation with a computer. "Good to know."

"What name shall I assign to your voice?"

"Sonny. My name is Sonny."

"How unique. My data bank does not include this name."

"Until now," I said.

"Indeed. I await your command, Sonny."

"Show me Bannar three days ago, please, Ellie."

Blue blinking lights covered the screen. I scrolled forward in time, until the screen vibrated, and red lights began vaguely flashing through a cloud of smoke and dust.

"Ellie, show me Rynstat one hour ago."

Two blue lights blinked back at me. "What the...?" *There should be three—Leolie, Pidge and me.* "Are you sure there are only two blue flashing lights?"

"Affirmative," Ellie said. "One for Leolie and one for Pidge."

"What about me? I was here one hour ago. Where's my flashing blue light?"

"I see your point. In my defense, Zardina programmed me. There is one chance in a quintillion that my program has an error."

"A quintillion?"

"All Astrobians know how to count by ions—million, billion, trillion, quadrillion, quintillion, sextillion—"

"Okay," I interrupted. "That's enough."

"You do not wish me to continue?"

"No. I get it. The chance of an error is very, very, very small."

I looked closer at the screen. The two blue lights were different—one brighter than the other. *Is Pidge's blue light the one that's fading because of a decrease of the enzyme in her system?*

"Ellie?"

"Yes, Sonny."

"Does the surveillance program track all life forms?"

"Only citizens. No animals, birds or insects."

"Only those beings with the W-35 enzyme?"

"That is correct. Logically, that would mean you do not have the W-35 enzyme."

That would explain why it can't see me. I sensed Bennett.

Hello, Sonny.

"Hey Bennett. Find anything?"

"I do not understand," Ellie said. "Find what?"

"Sorry. I was talking to someone else."

"But no one else is here, Sonny."

"Right. Well, just go into sleep mode for a while. I'll get back to you."

"Done," Ellie said. The screen went black.

"Bennett?"

Maybe. It's only a wild thought, but it looked like someone was stealing prized elements. You know, on Earth we call them 'rare earths.'

"Right. Rare earths. ... Used in all kinds of high-tech devices. Makes them lighter, smaller, and stronger."

Don't forget their applications in nuclear reactors and cancer treatments. Back home, extracting rare earths from minerals is a very costly process. But on Astrobia, they're readily available. No reason to steal them.

"So…what? You thinking someone from Earth got in through the portal and stole some rare earth rocks?"

Or, an alien from some other parallel universe.

"How would they get in and out?"

There is more than one portal. Perhaps they hacked the Astrobian computers.

"From their own planet? Their technology would have to be more advanced than Astrobia's."

Not necessarily.

"What do you mean?"

Zardina created portals between Astrobia and three other planets. The designs were ingenious. Each was developed using low frequency radio waves that matched the technology levels of the three different planets.

"How low?"

I am not certain, but I know it is even less than the cell phone frequencies used on Earth when I was taken.

"They may be ingenious, but the low frequency levels would be a major weakness."

Precisely. It's the 'Achilles heel' of her creation. So, let us suppose the aliens knew or suspected the existence of a portal?

"Like if an alien saw one of their own disappear through a transom window?"

Yes. But, unlike my grandmother who has no technology skills, what if the alien who witnessed the abduction was a scientist?

"That alien would be driven to figure out the underlying science."

Right. And maybe find a way to hack into the portal. They could have found a way to block the electro-magnetic sensors, as well.

"If we're correct, aliens might have been coming into Astrobia and leaving with prized elements for years."

But they should have been detected by the surveillance tracking system once they began travelling across Astrobia.

"That's what I thought. But I just learned that only Astrobians show up as a flashing blue light on the system's satellite observation level. It's all tied to the enzyme."

Really? That means aliens would be undetectable.

I nodded. "Of course, the general surveillance system was probably designed to monitor volcanoes and citizens, not aliens, right?"

Correct.

"You said it was possible to see a change in the electro-magnetic field if Pidge were traveling in the portal."

That's right.

"If I try to leave with Pidge, it'll probably be even easier to detect the change. That could get Leolie in big trouble."

Yeah. Big trouble. Doric has a reputation for becoming violent when his commands are disobeyed.

"What do you mean, violent?"

Remember he was the commanding general of the military when the volcanoes erupted. Then all of a sudden, he was the new Supreme Leader. From what I heard, no one got in his way. Nobody has since either.

"Not good for Leolie."

I am afraid not, if Doric finds out she has opened the portal in violation of a direct order.

"A diversion. Isn't that what Pidge said they needed?"

Yes. Something that would get people to turn their instruments away from the portal while she was in it.

"Seems like a great time for a volcanic eruption. I mean, just a little one. Enough to get everyone's attention, but not enough to hurt anyone."

That would do it.

"Are there volcanoes that look like they're ready to blow?"

The volcanoes here are like the ones on Earth—they could erupt any time. No reliable way to predict when. And it's certainly a waste of time hoping one would erupt precisely when Pidge would be in the portal.

"I wonder."

Twenty-Four

Sonny

"Ellie."

"Yes, Sonny."

"Stream video from the observation room. On zoom power."

The screen flickered on. According to the time and date, it was now the previous evening. The grounds were poorly lit, not able to see clearly.

I pointed. "What's that?"

Looks like a torvee, Bennett thought. *Kind of like our orangutans. The orange colored fur indicates a male. Actually, this is a rather large torvee. See. It's moving on all fours, but standing on its hind legs every once in a while. They tend to be shy, and stay in the forest. Rarely see them venture into populated areas.*

"Do they usually go inside the science building?"

Not a chance. Like I said, they are shy. Plenty of food in the surrounding forest.

"Well, that's what this one's doing."

My stars. You are right.

"What if our alien can imitate a torvee? Maybe it's a costume? Or a shape-shifter?"

Then it could easily move around without being discovered.

"And steal prized elements?"

Let's see when he comes out.

We watched the entire day in sped up time, until the explosion. But we never saw the torvee or any other non-Astrobian leave the building.

A few minutes later, the door to our chamber whooshed open. Pidge stood there, looking less energetic than when I first saw her, only an hour or so earlier. Her skin now a pale and blotchy green. Her purple hair was no longer bright.

She came in slowly, carrying a tray of colored objects with different shapes—round, tubular, almost rectangular, and one that was spiral like a continuous peel of an apple. She set the tray on the table.

"Expect your stomach is on lunch time," she said. "Eat these."

"What are they?"

"Astrobian fruits and vegetables."

"You look like you need these more than I do," I said.

Pidge forced a smile. "Do not think anything will help me now."

"Take me back to Earth with you, Pidge. Please."

Pidge looked surprised. "I do not know how you knew I would be trying to go back. But, no. I cannot take you, Sonny. I am sorry."

"Why not?"

"One, because I am not even sure I can make it. And two, Leolie cannot afford to let you go. The Supreme Leader would have her head for sure."

"What if there was a diversion?"

"A diversion," Pidge said with a sigh. "I do not think I can get out of Astrobia cleanly without a diversion. My being in the portal will create a change in the electro-magnetic force field that would be seen by others. And Doric clearly ordered Leolie not to allow anyone to leave Astrobia through the portal."

Pidge saw the monitor. "How did you...? You have seen the explosion?"

"Just trying to help."

"Trying to help? Help do what?" Pidge's eyes widened. "It is Bennett, right? He is the one who did this. He is the one who told you I would be trying to return to earth."

Tell her, Sonny. Bennett thought. *She is one of us.*

Pidge looked around. "He is here, right? Bennett is in this room right now."

I nodded slowly. "Please don't be mad. I thought if we could help Leolie with her investigation, then she'd have more time to work out how to get you...and me, back to Earth."

Pidge began to pace the small room. She stopped in front of me. "I cannot blame you. I would be doing the same thing. In fact, I am doing the same thing. But Leolie is my best friend. I cannot do anything that might harm her. If she does not have a solid diversion, I am not going."

Tell her that's exactly what you want too.

"Me too," I said softly. "I don't want anything to happen to Leolie."

Pidge swayed and her eyes rolled up. I grabbed her arm and led her to the chair.

Sonny, you've got to tell her everything. You may not have another chance.

I waited until Pidge recovered. "We think we've found something about the explosion."

Pidge looked up. "What?"

"Ellie."

"Yes, Sonny."

"Go back to the previous evening."

Pidge looked at the screen. "I have already seen this."

We watched as a male torvee appeared. "There," I said pointing.

"A torvee," Pidge said. "So what?"

"Just watch him."

Pidge sat up straight as the torvee stood on two legs and moved toward the building. "What the...? I must have looked away. I did not see it go inside."

I explained our thoughts about an alien hacking into the portal.

Pidge stood. "I must tell Leolie."

Don't let her leave until you tell her about your ideas for a volcanic eruption.

I touched Pidge's arm when she started to walk out. She turned to me.

"I have an idea about a diversion."

Twenty-Five

Bennett

I caught up to Pidge in the eating chamber, just as she sat down across from Leolie.

Leolie looked up. "You found an alien?"

Pidge nodded and told Leolie about finding the male torvee who did not act like a torvee. Then, without giving Sonny's name, presented his idea about the alien wearing a special torvee suit or possibly being a shape-shifter. She went on to explain his theory about hacking the system.

Leolie sat back without saying a word, but her eyes never left Pidge.

Pidge continued. "Our monitoring system is not designed to identify aliens, right?"

"That is correct. But how did you know this?"

"Because, when I dropped back to standard power, the alien did not register a flashing blue light. According to the system, the alien was no different than any animal."

Leolie said nothing.

"So?" Pidge asked. "What do you think? Could the portal system have been hacked?"

Leolie nodded slowly. "It could indeed. And you are correct about the very low frequency Zardina used to establish and maintain the portals. ... You say the alien never came out of the science building?"

"I never saw him again."

"So, if he set off the explosion it must have been an accident."

"It would make no sense for him to purposely set off an explosion because his mission was to get out of the building with the stolen elements."

"Okay," Leolie said. "I can tell Doric the explosion was an accident. But no telling what he would do if he found out aliens had hacked our portal system and had been stealing prized elements. That piece of information is best kept a secret."

"Do you know which portal the alien would have come through?"

Leolie shrugged. "Only Qetz the Great knows. I will reprogram all three of our portals at a more powerful radio wave frequency to make sure no more pirates get in."

"But not before you get me out. Unless you found Zardina's formula for the enzyme."

Leolie shook her head. "No way to read anything from her computer. And yes, I need to get you out first before I reprogram the portals. Now, show me the video. I want to see this for myself."

I floated behind them as Leolie helped Pidge to the observation chamber. Pidge called up the video. They watched the torvee in normal speed, then switched to a medium forward speed to monitor every being going in and coming out of the science building.

Leolie turned to Pidge. "Excellent work, my friend. An alien thief and an accidental explosion. Well done. Very well, indeed."

Pidge offered a forced smile. "Thank you. Now I have an idea about a diversion. One I think would work."

"Good. Tell me."

"A volcanic eruption."

"That is crazy. No way to predict that."

"What if we use a small volcano, like Lambou Mountain?"

"And what? Blow it up?"

"That is exactly what I was going to suggest. It has been rumbling for the last few months. And it is far away from civilization."

"Pidge. Is the drop in the W-35 enzyme messing with your brain?"

"Think about it. An explosive with a timer can be positioned just inside the mouth of the volcano. The timer would be set to match up with my entering the portal. All eyes would switch to the volcano. No one would be paying attention to the portals. They would never see me leave, and you would be in the clear."

"How do I get explosives to Lambou Mountain? I would be seen for sure."

"If you are okay with this plan, I will find a way."

"What do I tell Doric about what happened to you?"

"Just say I never recovered from my injuries."

Leolie stood. "Let me think for a minute."

"Do not take long. I do not have too many minutes."

Twenty-Six

Breanne

I looked at Mrs. Pidgeon. "What do we do now?"

Mrs. Pidgeon patted my hand. "Lorene and I've been through this before. When Bennett was taken, no one believed Lorene. The police assumed there was an Earth-based kidnapping and began an investigation. Even suspected Lorene had something to do with his disappearance. The principal thought she was out of her mind, and the school board wanted her to see a therapist."

"So, what happened?"

"Lorene stopped telling anyone that Bennett was pulled through the portal. ... Pidge was taken several years later, and Lorene was right by my side. We decided it would be best not to tell anyone. It was better that way. I never would have made it without Lorene."

It was my pleasure, dear," Mrs. Turner said.

I repeated her words for Mrs. Pidgeon.

Mrs. Pidgeon gave a tight lipped smile. "Even now, you are still helping me, Lorene."

"Well, *I* can't be quiet," I said. "I need to at least tell Sonny's grandmother. She knows about our skills, and she deserves to be told. Please, may I borrow your phone?"

"What happened to yours?"

"I don't have one. My mother says I'm not old enough yet."

Mrs. Pidgeon pulled an old flip phone from her purse and handed it to me. "It's old, but it's fine for making and receiving phone calls. Now I wouldn't try to send a text message because there's no keyboard—no single key assigned to each letter."

"Huh?"

She opened up the phone. "See? No typewriter keyboard, only numbers from one to zero, like the old house telephones. Look at the number two key. It has three letters on it: 'A, B, and C.' So, if you want to send a text that begins with a 'C,' you have to press the number 2 key three times before a 'C' shows up in the window."

"I don't get it."

"That's fine, sweetie. Don't worry about texting, just call her."

I opened my notebook computer and found Sonny's home phone number. I punched the large numbers on the flip phone.

"Hello," Mrs. Elliot answered.

"Mrs. Elliott, this is Breanne. Can you come to the school library?"

"Something's wrong. I can hear it in your voice. It's Sonny isn't it?"

"Yes, ma'am. But it'd be best to tell you in person."

"Be right there."

Twenty-Seven

Sonny

I paced the chamber. My brain was like a popcorn machine, ideas were exploding all over the place. I couldn't keep up with so many exploding kernels.

I need Bree. ... Too far apart to read each other's mind.

What would she do? ... Bree is always brave. She'd be looking at the big picture, trying to figure out how different things are connected. Be looking for ghosts to help us.

Bet she's already retraced my steps—going through the books in the library's science and math section, looking for clues.

Mrs. Turner's ghost will be watching the portal twenty-four/seven, looking for Bennett. And she'd tell Bree the second she sees anything.

They'll be waiting for me. How can I get outta here?

Blowing up a volcano for a diversion still sounds like a good idea. Pidge needs a diversion to protect Leolie, or else she won't go. And if Pidge ain't going, Leolie won't open Earth's portal from this side.

That means I'm here forever. Or at least for four years, like Bennett.

Pidge <u>has</u> to convince Leolie to blow the volcano.

How could she do it? Leolie's the only one who could plant the bomb. But her flashing blue dots will be seen by Doric as she travels to the volcano. Someone else has to put dynamite in the volcano.

Someone who can't be seen? That would only be me, or…Bennett.

As if on cue, I sensed Bennett's presence.

"Well? I said. "What's happening?"

Pidge told Leolie about your ideas, but did not mention your name. After watching the video, Leolie agreed about an alien possibly hacking the portal's low radio wave frequency and stealing the prized elements. She has gone to give her report to Doric in person. She will tell him the explosion was an accident.

"That's it?"

Leolie said she did not want Doric to know about the alien. And she would lock down all portals using an unhackable ultra-high radio frequency.

"The Earth portal, too?"

Yes, but she would wait until Pidge got out.

What about the volcano? She think blowing the volcano was a good idea?

Not really. But Pidge promised to work out a plan.

The door whooshed open. Pidge stood, holding on to
the door jamb. She steadied herself and slowly stepped
inside. I moved the chair closer to her. She lowered
herself into it, breathing hard.

*She is not looking so good, Sonny. Time is running
out.*

I waited for Pidge to speak.

She lifted her head, looked around. "I am assuming
Bennett is here with us, and that he has already told
you everything."

I nodded. "He's here."

Her breathing gradually returned to normal. "I need
your help on the volcano. I promised Leolie I would
have a plan, but I do not know how it could be done
without Doric's people catching us."

"Been thinking about that," I said. "First, I have to
ask Bennett a few questions."

Me?

"Yes, you. You said you can move objects."

Yes.

"How much weight can you carry?"

I don't know.

I pointed. "See if you can pick up that tray."

Pidge and I watched the tray rise about a foot above the table, then crash, spilling my lunch all over the floor.

Oops! Sorry.

"So, that's about as much weight as you can pick up?"

Guess so. Maybe it was just too hard to balance with all those rolling fruits and vegetables.

Pidge made a face. "What was that about?"

"I'm trying to see if there's any way Bennett can carry an explosive to that volcano."

What? Me? I don't know...

Pidge cocked her head, but didn't say anything.

"Bennett is able to move about Astrobia without being tracked. If he has the strength..."

Let's say I can do it. How would I be back in time to go through the portal with Pidge? This is my only chance. I have to get back home.

I repeated Bennett's words for Pidge, and then said, "We'd need a timer set so you could return to Rynstat before the volcano erupts."

"Can you, Bennett?" Pidge asked. "Can you drop an explosive into the mouth of Lambou Mountain for me? For us?" She looked at me expectantly.

Bennett didn't answer.

When I didn't say anything, Pidge shrugged and stuck her hands out in front pleading for an answer.

I held up my index finger as I concentrated.

Bennett's mind was all over the place, making it hard to read. *A bomb...What if I drop ... stupid tray? ...kill people. ...diversion...never happen. Pidge...refuse to go. Leolie...sealed shut forever.*

"Bennett," I said as calmly as I could. "Slow down. Let's think this through. ... Bennett?"

Yeah. ... Okay. Sorry.

"Can you think of a better way?"

Actually, I cannot. Your plan is off-the-wall brilliant— if it works.

I repeated Bennett's thoughts for Pidge.

She nodded. "I agree. 'Off-the-wall' is right. And if it does not work, Bennett and I will be keeping you company right here in Astrobia."

"Okay," I said. "Pidge can you put your hands on some explosives and a timer which is a whole lot lighter than this tray?"

Pidge nodded. "Weight won't be a problem. My problem is I do not think I can make it to the supply chamber by myself."

"I can help you," I said.

Pidge shook her head. "Not supposed to let you out. I will take Bennett."

"You're not thinking clearly," I said. "You can't hear him and he can't pick you up."

Ask her if she will let you take her if you promise to come back to this room with her.

"That's a crazier idea than the volcano," I said. "Why wouldn't I just run away?"

Really? Where would you go? And let us say Leolie opens the portal, how would you get to it if you are not here?

"Okay," I said, turning to Pidge. "How about I take you to the supply chamber and bring you right back here, where you can lock me up again."

"How can I trust you?"

"How can you not trust me? Without that volcanic eruption, you have no hope. None of us does."

"What does Bennett think?" she asked.

I sighed. "It's his idea."

"I guess I also have to trust you that it really is Bennett's idea."

"Come-on, Pidge. Clock's ticking."

Pidge stood and held out her barely green arm to wrap around my shoulder so I could help her walk out.

"Come with us Bennett," I said. "We want to make sure you can carry this. By the way, how long will it take you to fly to Lambou Mountain?"

Don't know. Never been out that far before.

Twenty-Eight

Sonny

Helping Pidge to the storage room felt like a weird dream. She's green with purple hair. Not like some kids back in Memphis who have streaks of purple. I mean really purple. And I'm on an unknown planet inside a windowless underground observation bunker where everything is made from some kind of metal—gray walls, gray floors, gray ceiling, gray doors. This was all messing with my brain.

Pidge pointed. "Just up here on the left."

The door whooshed open as soon as we passed in front of the beam.

I sat Pidge at a work table and she began giving me orders. "Get me that jar."

It contained a dozen or so tiny cylinders, about the size of a wooden match broken in half. Each had a thin wire hanging from one end. I assumed they were miniature detonators.

"I need one of those white tubes, they're lighter than the blue ones.

I grabbed one that was two-inches long.

"No," Pidge said pointing. "One of the really small white tubes, over there."

She opened a drawer and fished out a small digital timer, slightly larger than a dime. Then held her hand out. "Glue," she ordered.

I looked around, but did not see anything that looked like glue.

Pidge pointed at a small cylinder about the size of a spool of thread.

I picked it up. Shiny silver paper was wrapped around the spool. Clear colored drops were evenly spaced on the paper. It reminded me of those old fashioned candy dots on paper.

Pidge pulled one of the clear drops from the paper. "I must be careful. This is incredibly strong glue. I have only ten seconds from the time it leaves the special paper before it liquefies and bonds."

Using a tweezers-like instrument, Pidge placed the glue between the timer and the tube and held them together. Within seconds, a puff of white smoke appeared.

"Done," she said. "Nothing will break this bond, not even the explosion."

"What are you gonna use for the explosive?" I asked.

Pidge opened a container revealing blue cubes, smaller than our dice. She pulled out one cube and began rolling it between her hands like it was putty. She rolled it out until it looked like a blue worm, then stuffed it into the white tube. She pushed one end of the detonator into the putty and attached the detonator's wire to the timer.

"Done," Pidge said holding it up.

"I've seen higher tech bombs in Arnold Schwarzenegger movies," I said.

Pidge handed the miniature explosive to me. "Believe me, Arnold never had anything this powerful."

"Is it safe? Will it blow up if I drop it?"

Pidge laughed. "Not to worry, Mr. Scaredy-Cat. It would have to fall from a very high height to set if off. … Now for the big test. Let's see if it's light enough for Bennett to carry all that way."

I held out my open hand and watched the tiny bomb float up.

This will do just fine, Bennett thought as he lifted it up. *No problem at all.*

"Okay," Pidge said, working to get out of her chair. "You promised. Back to your chamber."

I let Pidge drape her arm over my shoulders and we headed back, following a floating bomb through the maze of gray hallways. Inside my chamber, we

watched the bomb float over and rest on the table. I
helped Pidge to the chair.

Twenty-Nine

Leolie

I took my time getting to the palace to meet Supreme Leader Doric. I needed to get everything straight in my head:

— Tell him I saw no evidence that would make me believe the explosion was anything but an accident.

— Do not tell him about Sonny. If Pidge's escape through the portal causes a disturbance in the electro-magnetic field, I will be able to say we had just captured Sonny. It was his coming into Astrobia that caused the disturbance. Having him here is essential to making this plan work. He will be *my* diversion.

— Do not say anything about Pidge being an Earthling.

— Do not say anything about aliens coming in and out of Astrobia to steal our prized elements. I will reprogram all the portals at the highest technological level to make sure no one gets in or out.

The palace came into view—a breathtaking, three-story, sparkling jewel perfectly set in the middle of a dense, green forest. The crystal building refracted the sunlight, sending multi-colored rays in all directions. A tall, rectangular wall of steel surrounded the palace. Years ago it was used to stop armed enemies. But now, the only danger came from an occasional wild animal, some every bit as large as the thick metal gate.

The gate opened as I approached. I flew my transporter inside, parked, and began the long walk to the palace itself. Female guards stood watch on either side of the tall double doors. Inside I was awestruck by the large statue of Qetz the Great that stood in the middle of the grand entrance hall. Large paintings and colorful tapestries covered the walls.

A man not much older than me approached, his facial expression flat and unreadable. He put his feet together and gave the slightest bow. I recognized his facial scar. He was the man I had seen standing behind Doric.

"I am Sittu," he said offering another slight bow. "Supreme Leader Doric is expecting you, Science Commander Leolie. You will follow me."

It had always been Science Commander Zardina. I am not ready for this. Get control. Being overly anxious would not be good. I must keep focused. I cannot afford to have any missteps. I worked to slow my breathing as I trailed after him.

Finally, Sittu led me into another massive chamber with what appeared to be a small stage on the far wall. On that stage, a man sat behind a large table—military-like jacket, long pants, and shiny boots—Doric.

His image always filled the video wall screen of Rynstat. I imagined him as being larger than any man I had ever encountered. But, with each step Doric appeared shorter. Even shorter than the typical Astrobian male. Much shorter than me. I could see the floor on his side of the table was a good foot higher than on my side of the table. It was his voice that was so large, so powerful.

He stood when we got closer. "Science Commander Leolie," he bellowed, as I climbed the three steps. "I am happy to finally meet you in person."

Once on the stage, I stopped and bowed my head, "Supreme Leader."

"Sit, sit," he said.

He remained standing until I sat down. Not, I believed, because he was being polite. Rather, because he wanted to appear taller.

"Please," he said. "Tell me what you have learned."

I cleared my throat and gave my report.

He leaned forward, his forearms on the table. "We are not under attack? Are you certain?"

"I saw no evidence of an attack, Supreme Leader."

He exhaled loudly and sat back. "Excellent."

No one spoke for several minutes. I heard the faintest of sounds and, without turning my head, glanced to the side. It was Sittu, shifting his weight from one foot to another. I did not realize he was still in the room.

"Honestly, Sittu," Doric said. "Can you not stand still for five minutes? You would make a terrible sentry in my military."

"Apologies, Supreme Leader," Sittu said as he bowed his head.

Doric turned to me. "Fortunately, Sittu has other talents I value."

I waited silently.

"I rely on him to monitor the planet," Doric said.

I must have raised my eyebrows.

"Oh, not like you do at Rynstat, Science Commander. No. He monitors people. He keeps tabs on what people are saying about me. Helps me know who my friends are. And who my enemies are."

"Enemies?" I said.

"Surely, you are not that naïve. All leaders have enemies. And all leaders must deal with them."

"Deal with them?"

"Let us hope I never have to show you my dungeon cells," he said smiling.

"You have a dungeon in this lovely palace?"

His voice turned serious. "I demand loyalty from my subjects, especially those subjects who have a leadership role under my rule. That now includes you, Science Commander Leolie."

I swallowed hard and gave a bow of my head.

"Now, tell me about these portals. Are they all closed? No one is leaving Astrobia, correct?"

The dead alien certainly will not be leaving. "No one is leaving Astrobia, Supreme Leader."

"And the new teenager?"

He knows about Sonny. "Sir?"

"When will you capture the new teenager?"

My heart pounded. "We will open the portal soon. Maybe even today."

"So we will have our alien teenager soon?"

"All we can do is put out the signals designed to attract the most talented teenager. Our signals are very powerful. But we cannot predict when we will have our capture."

"You must keep me informed."

"Yes, sir."

"I understand from Sittu that you were able to save one of the scientists at Bannar. Your friend Pidge, correct? Please give her my regards. We are in great need of every scientist."

Tell him how sick she is. "I will, Supreme Leader. But I am afraid Pidge did not come out of the explosion unscathed."

"Oh?"

"She is having medical problems. I fear they are serious."

Doric looked at Sittu. "You said nothing of this," he said, raising his voice. "You make me look like a fool."

"Truly, Supreme Leader. I confirmed she had been rescued and treated successfully. I knew nothing of any 'medical problems.'"

"I suggest any future assessment of her condition be conducted by you *personally.*"

Sittu bowed.

"See our guest out, Sittu," Doric said. "Then come back. We are going to have a little talk."

Sittu's eyes grew large. He bowed again, then turned to me. "Come."

Outside the Supreme Leader's grand chamber, Sittu slowed. "Tell me more of Pidge's 'condition.'"

"I am afraid she is quite ill."

"What exactly do you mean by 'quite ill?'"

"She has been losing consciousness. And her color is very bad."

"Bad color?" he asked.

"I have never seen anything like it. Her skin has turned a pale green."

"Where is she now?"

"I've been tending to her at Rynstat."

"I shall need to see her myself."

"Please let me know when you are coming so I can make sure Pidge is prepared to meet you."

Sittu stopped. "You will know when I walk through the door." He turned and headed back.

I quickened my pace, climbed into my transporter, and lifted off. Once out of sight of the palace I tapped my belt. "Leolie calling Pidge."

No answer.

"Leolie calling Pidge."

"Pidge here," she answered weakly.

"Prepare for a visitor from the palace. Be there in ten. Leolie, signing off."

Thirty

Bennett

Pidge looked at Sonny. "Trouble."

"The visitor?" Sonny asked.

Pidge nodded. "Whoever it is, they must not see you, or this bomb." She stood, slipped the bomb into her pocket and walked slowly across the room. Then she opened a short door to what appeared to be a very small storage closet and motioned to Sonny.

Sonny took a step back shaking his head. "No way. There's no room for me in there."

"Pidge motioned for him to come. "You can do it. Duck down, sit on the floor and get as comfortable as you can."

Sonny turned sideways and squeezed inside, slowly lowering himself to the floor.

Pidge looked down at him. "Promise me you will keep quiet. All our lives are in jeopardy."

"I promise," Sonny said. "Just don't forget to come get me when whoever-it-is leaves."

"I will not forget," she said.

Pidge waited for Sonny to move his foot back, then closed the door. She turned and walked slowly from the chamber.

Whoosh. Whoosh.

I floated through the closet door. Sonny was right. There really wasn't any room for him. That left even less room for me. I practically had to lie with my face on his head, and the rest of me hanging outside the door. *She's gone.*

Sonny groaned and squirmed. "I know," he whispered. "I heard the door."

She is right, you know. This is a big deal. The visit could ruin everything. What do we do now?

"We need information. Find out what's going on. How much time before the Earth portal is open? Then come back and tell me."

Be back...as soon as I know.

I found Pidge sitting in a chair in the observation chamber, catching her breath. She waved her hand across the console until she had pulled up a zoom shot of the palace on the wall screen.

Lots of different size transporters zipped in and out of the palace grounds, but none coming this way. She scrolled the picture back until she found Leolie's transporter parked outside Rynstat.

A door whooshed open and closed. I heard quick footsteps grow louder.

"Pidge," Leolie called.

"In here," Pidge said.

Leolie came in. "I could barely hear you on the radio. Tell me you are okay."

"Okay for a dying Astrobian," Pidge said. "What is all this about someone from the palace. Is the Supreme Leader coming?"

"No. One of his techie spies. A man named Sittu. Ever hear of him?"

Pidge shook her head. "Why is he coming?"

"Doric wants him to see how sick you are?"

"How does he know I am sick?"

"That is my fault," Leolie said. "I may have made a big mistake. But I was trying to let Doric know not to expect to see you around."

"I agree with your decision, but it still sounds strange that Sittu is coming out here."

"I think Doric was embarrassed that his number one spy had not given him the most up-to-date information on you."

"Let us hope he does not want to take me for a medical examination. That would really screw things up."

"You are going to have to pretend not to be too sick. Then maybe he will leave so we can get to work."

Pidge coughed several times, then caught her breath. "I will try."

"What about the teenager? Did you get him out of sight, somewhere Sittu will not find him?"

"Sonny is in the closet."

"That tiny storage half-closet in his chamber?" Leolie asked. "How did you squeeze him in there?"

"Told him if he was discovered, he would never get back to Earth."

"Why would he think he would be returning to Earth?"

"He is hoping to go with me."

Leolie shook her head. "No way. He is essential to the rebuilding of our scientific community. More than that, he is our diversion for opening the portal into earth."

"Huh?"

"If Sittu spots a shift in the electro-magnetic field, I will tell him it is because Sonny had just come into Astrobia through the portal."

"Sonny has been so helpful," Pidge said. "I thought the two of us could go back together."

"Impossible."

"He is really a bright kid. He is the one who spotted the alien sneaking into the Science Building."

"What? I thought you found the alien."

Pidge shook her head.

"Wait a minute. I am not following this. How did Sonny even see the video?"

"Here is where things get a little strange. Bennett is here too."

Leolie cocked her head. "Bennett? Not the Earthling Bennett Turner? He has been dead for about ten years."

"It is his ghost."

"Ghost? What nonsense is this? There is no scientific evidence for the existence of ghosts."

"That may be the case on Astrobia," Pidge said. "But there are ghosts on earth."

"How do you know?"

"Because Sonny told me. And he can read Bennett's mind."

Leolie put her hand on Pidge's forehead, checking her temperature. "Do you know how illogical you sound, Pidge? You are not making any sense. It must be the lack of the enzyme."

"I will prove it. Come with me to Sonny's room. I am sure Bennett will be there, and you can see for yourself."

Leolie turned to the console. "I have to keep tabs on Sittu."

"No. I insist." Pidge slowly stood and stretched out her arm for help. "Please."

Leolie sighed loudly. "Okay. But when I do not see Bennett, you have to promise to stop this foolish talk."

Thirty-One

Breanne

I waited at the main door for Sonny's Grams. Her car pulled up, the door flew open, and she practically ran to me. She reached up and grabbed my arms. Her eyes searched mine. "Tell me, child, what happened to my Sonny? Is he hurt? Is he hurt bad?"

Although barely five feet tall, I admit Sonny's grand-mother has always kinda scared me. Her internal strength and forceful nature made her appear much taller. But today was different. Today she seemed small and afraid.

"Come with me," I said escorting her to the library. "I don't think he's hurt. But I'm sensing that he's very frightened. It'll be easier to explain once we're in the library."

We hurried down the hall. I opened the door, but she hesitated when she saw the ladder. I guided her underneath it.

Mrs. Pidgeon came up and extended her hand. "Mrs. Elliott, I'm Marge Pidgeon, the school librarian. Please. Come sit down."

Grams looked up at me.

I nodded, and walked her to one of the large tables.

"Where's my Sonny?" she asked.

Mrs. Pidgeon took a deep breath. "Sonny was helping us, and then he was abducted."

"Abducted?" Grams asked. "Somebody took him? When? Are the police looking for him?"

"This is going to be very, very hard to explain," Mrs. Pidgeon said. "And even harder to understand."

"Well, somebody better get to explainin'," Grams said. "And right now!"

I touched her arm. "You know how sometimes Sonny and I see ghosts?" Grams nodded slowly. Then her eyes grew big. "You mean Sonny was disappeared by one of 'em polergizes?"

I had to think for a second. "Oh, no, ma'am. It wasn't a poltergeist. It's more like Alice in Wonderland. You know when she fell down the hole."

"Chasing after that white rabbit?"

"That's right. That hole is called a portal."

"Portal? Sonny used that word yesterday."

"It looks like we have a portal right here in this library," Mrs. Pidgeon said.

"You talkin' about the rabbit hole?" Grams asked.

"Not a hole to Wonderland," I said. "More like a hole to another planet."

Grams sat back in her chair. "Sweet Jesus."

Mrs. Pidgeon leaned forward. "Years ago my niece Pidge and Mrs. Turner's grandson Bennett were sucked through that transom window," she said pointing. "Your Sonny was sucked through the same window today. Breanne and I held on to his ankles as long as we could. But the pull was too strong and we could not keep him from being taken."

Grams turned to me in disbelief.

I nodded and took her hand in both of mine.

"What can we do?" Grams asked. "There must be something."

Mrs. Pidgeon looked down at the table. "Sixteen years ago, Lorene watched Bennett get pulled through that transom window. No one believed her. The police even suspected she had something to do with Bennett's disappearance."

She paused, then looked up. "Heck, even though Lorene and I got to be good friends, I didn't believe her either. Not until I watched the same thing happened to my niece. When that happened, Lorene was the only one who believed me."

"So, that's it?" Grams said. "We don't tell anyone because no one will believe us? We just wait?"

"Afraid so," Mrs. Pidgeon said, looking up at the transom window. "Lorene's spirit waits up there, and I wait down here. Today was our first glimmer of hope when Bennett's ghost showed up at the transom window. Even though it was the ghost of a very old man."

"He's been trying to get back through the portal," I said. "And Sonny talked to him."

"Sonny talked to him?" Grams asked.

I nodded. "Now we know Sonny won't be alone. He'll have Bennett, and maybe Pidge, too."

"The three of them are so intelligent," Mrs. Pidgeon said. "I have to believe they'll find a way back. And sooner, rather than later."

Thirty-Two

Breanne

Waiting is terrible—not knowing what's happening to Sonny.

Is he hurt? Is he alive? When will he come back? Will he ever come back?

The grownups had stopped talking long ago. For the third time, Mrs. Pidgeon is checking to make sure every library book had been shelved in its correct place.

All I could hear was the quiet ticking of the wall clock. It was kinda soothing. I realized I was rocking side-to-side to its rhythm.

I felt her eyes before I looked up. Grams was totally focused on my face. Not like she was staring. It was more like she was trying to read my expression.

"You can hear him, can't you?" Grams said quietly. "You can hear Sonny."

I shook my head. "Not hear him. But I can sense him. His moods."

"Tell me."

"He's scared. Very scared."

"Dear Lord, I feel him, too," Grams said. "Like he's callin' me to help him. But I feel helpless. I don't know what to do."

"I've been trying to stay calm and concentrate. Hoping maybe he can sense me, too. If so, my being calm might help him."

"Sonny's really smart ain't he? I mean book-learnin' smart."

I nodded. "Don't know anyone smarter in science and math."

"But not so much in people smarts."

"People smarts?"

"Yeah. He can carry on with adults all right. But ever since he was little, Sonny didn't fit in with other kids. I'd go up to the school and he'd always be off by himself. Got to where he wanted to be alone all the time. Far as I know, he never even had a friend. Not till you come along. You've been good for him."

I felt my cheeks get hot. "Thanks. Actually, we're kind of alike. Sonny's my first friend, too."

"I remember the first time I met you," Grams said. "You came to my house with your grandfather."

"My grandpa was investigating Sonny's report of seeing one teenage boy shoot another boy."

"Sonny was having trouble remembering what he saw in that thunderstorm," Grams said.

I nodded. "Because what Sonny had seen was a ghostly recreation of an old murder."

"But then you touched his hand and his memory was clear as a bell. How'd you do that?"

"I can't explain it. When we touched, both of us saw everything clearly. But it's not something I did by myself. It was something the two of us did together."

Grams stayed quiet, like she was thinking about what she was going to say. "Did Sonny tell you that my grandmother used to hold séances and contact spirits?"

"Yeah. He said you used to sit in on the séances."

"A few of 'em. ... Always wished I could be like Grammy. But looks like all her spirit skills skipped over me *and* my son, then went straight to Sonny."

"Maybe you have some of her abilities, too," I said.

"Think so?"

"Makes sense. I don't see how all your Grammy's special gifts would jump over you and Sonny's father without leaving y'all some."

Grams thought about that for a while, then asked, "Think if we held hands, we could contact Sonny?"

"I don't know," I said, holding out both hands, "but let's try."

Grams took my hands. "What do we do now?"

"Close your eyes and concentrate on Sonny."

Almost immediately, I could feel the difference. It was like Sonny was at the opposite end of the building. Or maybe, he was at the other end of the portal. I focused my concentration on the transom window.

"We did it!" Grams whispered loudly. "I can feel him. He's really scared."

Thirty-Three

Sonny

I forgot how to breathe. I've never been this scared.
My whole body tingled with fear—like having a gazil-
lion little electrical shocks.

Like standing on the white line in the middle of the
expressway with eighteen-wheelers coming in both
lanes, one right after the other. Feeling the wind from
the huge speeding truck in the right lane blow me
closer to the one on the left. Believing the next truck
would hit me for sure. I tried to scream, but my mouth
was so dry nothing came out.

I started to hear things. *Grams? Is that you?*

"Can't just be a cry-baby. You gotta beat this. Use
your brain, child."

I can't think. I'm terrified.

"Have to be like your father, a Marine in Afghanistan. Don't let fear stop you. Figure a way out."

162

A way out? Look at me. Kidnapped. Stuffed inside this shoebox of a closet on another planet. I'll never get back home.

"You back-sassing me, child?"

No, ma'am. I'm just... I mean, I can't...

Then I heard it. First, softly in the distance, but getting louder.

Luciano Pavarotti. Singing *Nessun Dorma,* my favorite opera piece. Momma played opera from the time I was in her womb 'til I was one-year old. That's when her Air Force unit was called up to fight in Afghanistan...Momma never came home, killed when her Humvee ran over an IED—an improvised explosive device. Grams said Momma played opera all the time because she thought it would make me smart.

Momma? Is that you? Are you playing Pavarotti for me? Are you and Grams telling me to use my brain? I'll try.

So hard to concentrate. I can't feel my toes and my thoughts are just bouncing around inside my head:

I wonder what time it is back on Earth? Grams would probably be starting dinner.

My shoulder hurts like mad.

Any way Bree can hack into the portal?

Can't move. My ear itches. But...I can't reach it.

Not hap'nin'. Bree doesn't know anything about hacking.

How long am I supposed to stay here twisted like a pretzel?

Whoosh. Whoosh

My eyes snapped open. Footsteps. *Is that the palace guy? Is he in my chamber? ... Don't make a sound.*

The steps came right up to the closet door.

The door opened. Light from the room blinded me. I felt strong hands grab me. I kept blinking to get used to the light. It was Leolie.

She pulled me up, but I couldn't stand. I had no feeling in my legs. She dragged me over to the chair.

Leolie picked up Pidge and sat her on the table. "How long have you had him locked up in there?"

"I don't know," Pidge said. "Right after you radioed."

I kept stretching my arms and moving my legs. Gradually, feeling returned in my feet and hands, like hundreds of bees stinging me.

"Has he gone?" I asked.

Pidge shook her head. "He hasn't even shown up yet."

Leolie kept a hand on Pidge's shoulder to steady her, then turned to me. "Pidge has been talking nonsense. I need you to tell me the truth."

"It's okay, Sonny," Pidge said. "Tell her everything."

"What's all this about Bennett being a ghost, and you being the only one who can talk to him?" Leolie asked.

"Actually, anyone can talk to Bennett. He hears us clearly. It's just that we can't hear him. But I can read his mind."

"Enough!" Leolie shouted. "I said the truth!"

"It's the truth," I said. ... "Bennett?"

I am here.

"Leolie needs proof," I said, pointing. "Take that flashlight off her belt."

All eyes went to the small gray flashlight. We heard the Velcro rip open, then watched the flashlight rise and float to me. I took it.

"Thanks, Bennett."

"What kind of trick is this?" Leolie demanded.

I shook my head. "It's not a trick. You may not have ghosts on Astrobia, but we do on Earth. Very few Earthlings can communicate with ghosts. I'm one of them."

"Now will you believe me?" Pidge asked.

Leolie shook her head, pointed at me. "He is some kind of magician."

"Bennett's the one who told me the portals were developed using low communications frequencies," I said. "How would I know that?"

"Even I didn't know that, Leolie," Pidge said.

"Okay," Leolie said. "Does <u>Bennett</u> know why they were programmed that way?"

Certainly. In those days, the portals could not be established without matching the lower radio wave frequency levels being used on Earth and the other two parallel planets.

I told Leolie and Pidge what Bennett told me.

Leolie's mouth dropped open.

"I asked Bennett to help investigate the explosion at Bannar," I said. "He was with you in the supply bay when you brushed the floor with your fingers to check the silvery dust."

"From the prized elements," Leolie murmured.

"Now do you believe me?" Pidge asked.

Everyone jerked when we heard a distant whoosh.

"He's here," Leolie said quietly.

A second whoosh.

"Quick," Leolie pointed. "Sonny, back in the closet. Pidge. In the chair."

I squeezed into the closet, too scared to feel the pain of being refolded and stuffed inside. Leolie hurried over and used her boot to force my shoes inside. Then I felt her muscle the door closed against my shoulder until the latch clicked.

I heard the double whoosh of my chamber's door and assumed Leolie had left to meet the palace guy.

Thirty-Four

Bennett

I left before Leolie. I wanted to see this Sittu—the visitor—myself. I found him in the observation chamber studying the console.

Leolie came in. "I see you have found the heart and soul of Rynstat."

Sittu turned. "Yes. Impressive. I believe your equipment is even more advanced than mine."

"It was built with the most powerful technology of the time, and is upgraded regularly. Protecting the planet is an important assignment, would you not agree?"

"It is indeed. Almost as important as my job."

"You mean spying on people?" Leolie asked.

"Protecting the Supreme Leader by letting him know who he can trust and who he cannot."

"What an odd job."

Sittu raised his eyebrows. "And you, Science Commander? Can he trust you? Did you tell the Supreme Leader everything?"

"I have given him no reason to doubt my trustworthiness."

"I don't think you convinced him. That is why I am here."

"Me? You are watching _me_?"

"You should know, Science Commander, I am always watching. Now, where is this Pidge person? I must see her condition for myself."

"Come," Leolie said as she turned and headed for the chamber.

Sittu hung back. I saw him take something from his pocket and hide it under the lip of the console before following Leolie.

I zipped through the walls and arrived in the chamber just before the door whooshed open. Leolie entered and went straight to Pidge, still sitting at the table. Her skin now even more pale green with patches of her Earthly freckled skin exposed. And strands of her Earthly red hair showed in her fading purple hair.

Sittu took two steps inside, saw Pidge and stopped. He made a face and pointed a green finger at her. "I have never seen anything like that. Is she contagious?"

Leolie put her hand on Pidge's shoulder. "I do not think so. The explosion unleashed a great number of chemicals. She is most likely having a reaction to one or more of them."

Sittu backed up, as if he believed his health was in danger. "I will report her condition to Doric." He turned to leave. "Remember, Science Commander, I will be watching."

The door whooshed closed.

I immediately poked my head through the closet door. *Be careful, Sonny. Do not speak. Do not move. We are being monitored. Sittu left some kind of device in the observation room, under the lip of the console. If you can read my thoughts, tap softly on the closet door.*

Leolie looked up when she heard Sonny's light tapping, and walked over to the closet. She started to open the door, but Sonny caught it part way, startling Leolie. She looked inside. Sonny put his finger against his puckered lips and shook his head.

Leolie seemed confused. "What the—"

"That dumb door," Pidge interrupted loudly, as she quickly struggled off the chair and stumbled over to Leolie. "It has been sticking," she said, breathing heavily. "Maybe the two of us can figure it out."

Leolie, still holding the door handle, stared at Pidge.

Pidge took Leolie by the arm and pushed her face into the closet. "Here. You look inside while I jiggle the door from the outside." Pidge moved between the computer screen and the door. "See if you can find where it is catching."

Leolie was inches from Sonny's face. That's when Sonny whispered what I had told him. Leolie jerked away, her eyes wide, then turned to Pidge. "I think I see the problem, but first I need to get something from the observation chamber. Be right back. Don't move."

Whoosh. Whoosh.

Leolie was gone.

The door whooshed open only a minute later. Leolie walked in carrying something about the size of a raisin. She held it up to the light then brought it down for closer inspection.

The computer screen blinked on. Pidge pointed at a real-time picture of Leolie looking at the device.

Leolie closed her fingers in a fist around the device, and her picture left the screen. She looked at Pidge. "Will someone please enlighten me? How did you know what was going on?"

"I could tell Sonny was concerned," Pidge said. "A finger over puckered lips is an Earthling signal to be quiet."

"Quiet?"

Pidge nodded. "I knew you'd never seen it before because Astrobians don't use that signal. And with Sittu's last words telling us he'd be watching, I figured maybe that's what Sonny was warning us about."

"Quick thinking," Leolie said. "But how did Sonny know? ... Oh. Bennett."

Pidge nodded, then pointed at Leolie's fist. "Now we know what Sittu meant by, 'I will be watching?' But I don't understand why."

"He said Doric does not trust me."

"Something you did? Something you said?"

Leolie shook her head. "Not sure. Maybe I was too nervous when I gave my report. Maybe he's just very suspicious."

"Talk about trust," Pidge said, "Sittu is not a man to be trusted. On earth, we would call him a 'slime ball.' He is so sneaky, hiding that <u>thing</u> in our work area. So, what the heck is it?"

"It is a data collector. Never seen one this small. Probably designed to spy on all our data—video, atmospheric readings, seismographic data, even our conversations."

"You need to be careful, Leolie. What are you going to do?"

Leolie opened her fist, let the data collector drop to the floor, and then crushed it with her boot heel.

Pidge rocked back in her chair. "He'll know what you did."

"He already knows I have it," Leolie said, pointing behind her. "Ellie just told him."

"Yeah, but when he comes back here, what will you say?

"I do not like anyone spying on me, and I will tell him so."

Thirty-Five

Sonny

Leolie pulled me from the closet.

Again, I shook my limbs from their 'sleep.' I must've looked like I had ants in my pants. Actually, it kinda felt like that, except the ants were inside my skin.

When I stopped moving, Leolie said, "Thank you, Sonny. You will make a great addition to our science community."

I shook my head. "Addition? No. I wanna go home."

"I cannot do that. Especially with Pidge leaving. Astrobia is too vulnerable. I will need every scientist I can get."

I don't know what happened. Hope left me, like air hissing out of a punctured tire. All my muscle strength left me. My knees buckled, and I collapsed to the floor in a heap.

The next thing I remember, Pidge was on the floor beside me with her arm wrapped around my shoulders. "I am sorry," she whispered. "But my time is running out. You have to tell Leolie about the diversion plan."

I had no energy, but when I looked at Pidge, I was quickly filled with concern. You didn't have to be a doctor to see she was in really bad shape. I couldn't let her instantly grow old and die. And I did not want Leolie to be in trouble. So, I told Leolie about our plan, and suggested she choose the time for the eruption.

Leolie nodded. "Sittu will be watching the portal so closely now. He will be able to tell if any change in the electro-magnetic field is caused by someone coming in, or by someone leaving Astrobia. Blowing up a volcano is a very unconventional plan, but I do not know what else to do."

Pidge pulled the tiny bomb from her pocket and gave it to Leolie.

"Okay, Bennett," Leolie said. "How long will it take you to get to Lambou Mountain and back?"

Been thinking about that. No population areas, so there should be no air traffic to dodge. I estimate I can make it there in thirty minutes. Then another half-hour to get back here.

I repeated Bennett's thoughts.

"Pidge cannot wait any longer. I'm setting the timer for Two-fifteen," Leolie said. "That will give you ten minutes extra. But you must leave immediately."

We all watched as the bomb floated in the air. *Some-one will need to open the door. I can get out easily, but this bomb will not pass through the walls.*

As soon as I repeated Bennett's thoughts, Leolie strode from the room. In the distance, Pidge and I heard the whoosh of the outside door. Seconds later, a second whoosh, followed by the sound of Leolie's footsteps.

"Sure weird seeing that floating bomb," Leolie said.

I heard Pidge whisper something but couldn't hear what she said. I bent down to get closer.

"Help me up," Pidge managed to whisper.

I tried, but she was too weak to help. I couldn't do it. Leolie quickly came over, slipped her arms under Pidge and scooped up her limp body.

"Come on," Leolie said to me. "The portal chamber."

Once inside the portal chamber, she gently laid Pidge down in the center of the room, on the exact spot where I had landed earlier in the day. The same spot where I first met Pidge. She looked so different now.

Leolie turned to me, still holding Pidge's hand. "Stay with her. Call to me the second she…" Tears filled Leolie's eyes. She looked at Pidge, then back at me. "Let me know immediately if there are any changes."

I nodded. "I'll watch her."

"Be strong, Pidge," Leolie said as she stood. "I must program the portal so you can get back to Earth. Bennett will be back soon."

Thirty-Six

Bennett

Carrying the bomb is going to be tricky, especially over a long distance. In my spirit form, I can't really grab objects or push them because I would simply pass right through them. It has more to do with generating a kind of force field just beyond my fingers. More like what happens when one bar magnet pushes away another bar magnet with the opposite pole.

It takes concentration and lots of practice. I have to get my hand near the object and focus my energy against it. It is almost like willing the object to move. So, I slip my hand under the bomb and force it to float just above my hand.

Lucky, it is not very windy this afternoon. I am making good time, passing over forests, foothills, and now a river. I caught movement high above me. An ulclan.

Not too different from our falcon. Excellent vision. High flyer. Incredible speed. And always on the look-out for food. It can probably see the bomb from way up there, even though the bomb is smaller than an Earthly humming bird. I wonder if it's big enough for the ulclan to consider it to be a meal. It is getting closer. Oh, geez. It has its wings back. It is diving right at the bomb.

Steady...steady. Now! Pull the bomb back.

Zoom!

The ulclan flew right through me, claws first. It did not get the bomb, but the wind created by the ulclan's speed forced it to pop up well above my hand, beyond my ability to control it.

Nooo...Must get the bomb before it hits those rocks down there and explodes!

I dove behind the bird. The ulclan had been going so fast it was way ahead of the falling bomb which was heading straight for an outcrop of boulders.

The bomb would explode on impact. An explosion out here in no-man's land would not generate any interest. And it would not attract Sittu's or his computer's attention away from monitoring the portal. And most certainly, it will not cause the volcano to erupt. Then Pidge will refuse to enter the portal, and I will never get home.

I put on more speed, and was closing the gap when I saw the ulclan circling back for another run.

I stretched and slid my hand underneath the bomb, only feet above the rocks. I twisted upright, but my momentum carried me feet first deep inside one of the large boulders.

I reached up to keep the bomb over my head and away from the boulder.

I stopped just as the bomb came to rest gently on top of the boulder.

I had never been inside anything as dense as a boulder. I felt a little claustrophobic. But, thankfully, the bomb did not explode.

Then I remembered the ulclan.

I pushed up from the boulder, raising the bomb above my head just as it came screaming at me from the left. I made one more push and the ulclan passed clean through me, but under the bomb.

Again, the wind from the bird sent the bomb sailing away from me. I zipped over and caught it before it hit another boulder.

This time the ulclan continued to fly away. But now, I am behind schedule. I can actually see Lambou Mountain and the large fluffy white clouds covering the top. But I do not think I can get there within my thirty-minute timeline.

I gathered myself and flew as fast as I could, keeping an eye out for another ulclan. I am a scientist, but I do not know anything about explosives. I began worrying if the moisture in the clouds would turn the bomb into a dud. No way for me to protect it, and no turning back now. I can only continue.

Thirty-Seven

Sonny

Pidge looks like she's dying.

A wave of panic washed over me.

I don't know what to do. ... I thought I heard Breanne—way in the distance.

Breathe, Sonny. Calm down. Can't think when you're so scared.

Bree? That really you?

Yes. Me and your Grams are here.

Pidge is passed out. I don't know what to do, Bree. I don't know how to help her.

Remember that paramedic who came to school and talked about life saving?

Yeah. Sorta. Let me think. ... CPR ... Pretty sure he said only give CPR if the person is <u>not</u> breathing. But Pidge is breathing. So, no CPR.

She bleeding? Breanne asked.

No. But she looks so uncomfortable. Maybe I should get something to rest her head on.

No, wait, Sonny. What was that stupid little poem. The one he made us say over and over.

Let's see... it has to rhyme. 'When the face is pale ... raise the tail.'

Yeah, that's it. I thought. *And 'when the face is red, raise the head.'*

Yes. So, what's her face look like?

It's really pale. So I need to raise the tail—that means raise her feet—so she can get more blood to her head.

I scanned the room for something to put her feet on. I saw a little two-step stool. I pulled it over and put Pidge's feet on the second step. "Okay. Her feet are elevated." I dropped to one knee beside her head. "Now let's see if the color returns to her face."

I heard running. The door whooshed open and Leolie burst into the chamber. She started to speak but froze when she saw Pidge.

Leolie looked at me and cleared her throat. "Got a problem, Sonny. A big problem."

"What?"

"Can't open the portal to Earth. The program is not responding."

I stood up. "But Lambou Mountain is going to erupt in less than an hour."

"You do not think I know that? I need help."

"I don't know anything about your portals."

"But you are a good problem solver, Sonny. Help me solve this problem. Why can I not open the portal?"

I struggled to switch gears from Pidge to the portal. "Okay... Well, have you had this problem before?"

"Actually, I have only ever opened the portal leaving Earth and coming into Astrobia. Like when it pulled you in. I have never opened a portal for leaving Astrobia. All three portals leaving Astrobia have been closed for years."

"Were the commands programmed the same way?"

Leolie nodded.

"Anything happen in the last few years that would've changed the commands?"

Leolie shrugged. "I do not know. Only Zardina worked on that."

Then it hit me. "Any chance you can't get through because the aliens who hacked the portal, changed some of the commands so they couldn't be blocked from leaving?"

"Brilliant, Sonny. That must be it."

"But you don't know what their commands are."

"True," Leolie said, her eyes open wide. "But I know the command to open one side of the Earth portal. I should be able to rewrite that command to open the other side as well."

Leolie spun around and ran out.

I looked at the wall clock and called after her, "You only have forty-three minutes!"

Thirty-Eight

Bennett

I made my way up Lambou Mountain. Going through the clouds was like passing through a fellow spirit—I couldn't see anything but ghostly white, and I got a slight chill. Finally, I reached the top. This volcano must have erupted years ago because its peak has been completely blown off. Nothing but an open crater now.

Rising hot air blew right through my face as I came over the edge of the crater. I could see molten lava bubbling at the base of the crater. This volcano is not far from blowing on its own. It just needs a little help.

The hot air current was not strong enough to carry the little bomb from my hand. But it made balancing the bomb difficult, and it forced me to descend more slowly than I wanted to.

I kept checking the sides for a ledge where I could place the bomb. The lower I got, the hotter it was. I had to leave the bomb low enough for the explosion to cause the volcano to erupt. But not so low the intense heat would trigger a detonation before the Two-fifteen deadline.

I went as far down as I dared, then positioned the bomb on a ledge. The timer read One-fifty. I only had twenty-five minutes to get back to Rynstat, or I'd miss going through the open portal. *Why did I ever agree to do this?*

Thirty-Nine

Leolie

I hurried to the computer and opened the basic portal program. It had been written in an old computer programming language, one that was used years ago, well before my time. I reduced that screen and conducted a search for computer programming languages. I began toggling between the existing portal program and old programming language descriptions until I found the right language.

From there it was a matter of getting familiar with the old programming language used to develop the portal. I modified the existing program so I would be able to open the portal leaving Astrobia and entering Earth. Now I needed to wait until Lambou Mountain erupted.

I jumped when the large wall screen flashed. A split second later Doric's face filled the wall.

I bowed my head. "Supreme Leader."

"Science Commander Leolie," Doric said. "Glad I found you. Sittu just told me about his visit to Rynstat."

Oh-oh. Here it comes. "Sir?"

"Pidge. He told me about Pidge."

Sittu didn't tell him about the data collector? That is a relief. "Pidge is not doing well."

"Not well? According to Sittu's description, her skin is peeling away and she can barely sit up."

I nodded. "I am very concerned."

"As am I. I have been planning for Pidge to take your place."

What? Take my place? "Sir?"

"That way Rynstat would be in capable hands."

He's relieving me of my position because I did not anticipate the explosion? "Yes...your eminence."

"Zardina was my most trusted advisor. She had great confidence in Pidge. It was Zardina who recommended Pidge for this promotion."

But Zardina appointed me to oversee Rynstat. Why did she change her mind? Why did she not tell me? "I see..."

"I don't think you do."

"Sir?"

"I am getting on in years. I need to select a replacement. Someone highly skilled. Someone the people can respect. Someone we can all trust to lead Astrobia for years to come."

No. Not Sittu. Who could trust him? I nodded.

Doric cocked his head and stared off, as if thinking. "Someone who would begin as my second in command."

I waited for Doric to continue.

He looked into the camera. "So? What do you think?"

"I can stay here as long as Pidge is ill."

"Yes. Yes, of course. ... I agree. Give me regular updates on her progress."

"Yes, Supreme Leader."

The screen went black.

I was dumbfounded. *What just happened? Maybe Doric is mad because Sittu did tell him about my crushing his data collector. But he said Zardina had already recommended Pidge take my place? When did that happen? What did I do wrong? Did Pidge know about this?*

I went back to the portal chamber. Pidge was still lying on her back with her feet on the stepstool. Sonny sat on the floor beside her. He looked up.

"You figure it out?"

I nodded. "How is she?"

Sonny looked down at her. "Well, her face is not as pale as it was and she's breathing better. But she hasn't opened her eyes or said anything."

I pointed. "What are those spots on her face and arms? And her hair?"

"Yeah, red hair is replacing some of the purple. Men and women on earth have different color hair—brown, black, yellow, gray, or red. Looks like Pidge was a red-head. Those with red hair usually have these spots on their skin. It's not a disease. They're called freckles."

"Freckles?"

"Yeah."

"No disease? You are certain?"

He shook his head. "Just means she's becoming her old self again."

"I did not know her before she took the enzyme. ... Red hair. Cream color skin. Freckles. Even her colorful chakata tattoo now has freckles. She really looks... different."

Sonny glanced down at her. "Real different."

I dropped to one knee beside her. "Pidge. Can you hear me?"

Pidge moaned. Moved her head a little.

"Pidge? It is me, Leolie. Can you hear me?"

"Leolie," Pidge mouthed, but no sound came out. She slowly licked her lips. "Leolie," she whispered with a soft breath.

I took her hand. It was limp. "Yes. It is me. The portal program is ready. Twenty-one more minutes before the eruption."

Pidge blinked open her eyes. "So weak," she whispered. "Feel strange."

"The effects of the enzyme are wearing off. Your body is returning to its Earthly form. You will begin to age soon."

"Must go...Earth."

"I know. I will send you. But in your present condition, I do not know if you can withstand the pressure of traveling through the portal tunnel."

"Have...to...try."

"Pidge? Did Zardina say anything to you about taking over command of Rynstat?"

Freckles bunched together on Pidge's forehead as she made a face. "Wha...?"

"Did Zardina tell you she wanted you to take over command of Rynstat?"

"That is...your...job."

She did not know anything about it. I smiled, and laid her hand gently on her stomach.

Forty

Breanne

Grams sighed. "I lost contact. How 'bout you?"

I shook my head. "Nothing. Maybe he moved farther away. Or maybe he just calmed down, 'cause I'm not sensing his fear right now. I'm not sensing anything from Sonny."

Grams looked at me with tired eyes that made her seem very old. "I so want to believe he's not afraid."

"Me too."

"This is exhaustin', ain't it?"

"We can try again later."

Grams nodded.

I felt her hands relax. We let go and faced the table side by side, but alone.

The quiet echoed in my ears. I looked at the clock— almost two. It felt like forever ago since Sonny was sucked through the portal. Fatigue came over me like a rolling ocean wave—first my mind, then my body.

My arms and shoulders felt so heavy. I let my hands drop into my lap, and I slumped forward. *Sonny's gone.*

My eyes welled up. Everything seemed out of focus. The table blurred as it moved side-to-side. I blinked to clear the tears and take a better look. It was not the table that moved. It was me. I was swaying to the rhythm of the soft ticks of the wall clock.

"What in the world?" Mrs. Pidgeon said, breaking the silence.

I jerked alert and looked up. I found the top of Mrs. Pidgeon's head above the rows of books.

"What is this book doing out of place," Mrs. Pidgeon said. "I've checked the books twice. It wasn't out of place before."

I scooted my chair back and went to see what she was talking about. I found her in the Science/Math row, holding a small red book.

She held it up. "A New Look at an Old Question," she said, turning the book over to read the back cover. "It's about something called 'string theory.'"

"Sonny knows about that," I said, holding out my hand. "May I see it?"

"Of course," Mrs. Pidgeon said, handing it to me.

As soon as I opened the book I felt this overwhelming urge to look at the transom window.

The next thing I remember I was on the floor. I couldn't move. I opened my eyes to a blurry world. *My glasses. Where are my glasses?* I struggled but couldn't move. Someone was on top of me with their arms tightly wrapped around my waist. I made out the top of Mrs. Pidgeon's head. She was practically sitting on my feet. She kicked hard, and a red book slid across the floor.

"Don't let go," Mrs. Pidgeon grunted, as if she were out of breath.

"I got her," said Grams. "She ain't goin' nowhere."

I struggled to move my arms and legs. "What're you doin'? Get offa me."

"Not till you start actin' right," Grams said.

"What are you talking about? Let me up."

"Are you back with us, dear?" Mrs. Pidgeon asked.

I struggled again, but couldn't budge. "Back from where?"

"What do ya think, Marge?" Grams asked.

"I think we let her sit up," Mrs. Pidgeon said, "but don't let go of her until we are certain."

I sat up. Grams sat behind me, her arms still wrapped around my waist. Mrs. Pidgeon had a vice grip on my ankles, one in each hand.

"Will someone tell me what's going on," I demanded.

Mrs. Pidgeon nodded with her chin in the direction of the red book. "It all happened when you opened that book. Took me forever to pry it from your hands. You don't remember?"

"You talking about that little red book? The one you misfiled? I never opened it."

"Afraid you did," Mrs. Pidgeon said. "And as soon as you did you took off running to the ladder."

Grams loosened her grip. "Marge yelled for help. Said you were heading for the portal. Said to stop you. So, I did. Tackled you right here."

"I'll say," Mrs. Pidgeon said, smiling. "As good a tackle as any pro football player."

"I twisted around to look at Grams. "You tackled me?"

"Yup. And I'll do it again if need be."

My left shoulder throbbed. I reached over to rub it. "I don't remember any of this."

"Must be something about that book," Mrs. Pidgeon said. "You told me Sonny knew about string theory. Maybe he was looking at this same book when he was drawn to the portal."

"You think that book is how Sonny, Bennett, Pidge and I were drawn to the portal?"

"Possibly," Mrs. Pidgeon said. "That, and y'all being as intelligent as you are. Good thing you never made it up to the portal. We'd never have been able to keep you from getting sucked inside like they were."

"Will someone please find my glasses?"

Forty-One

Bennett

I zipped out of the crater, through the clouds, and away from the mountain. The air currents had increased, so I dropped down to tree-top level. I passed over the foothills and was crossing the river when I was stopped, smack over the middle of the water.

"What the...? How can this be?

I spun around.

I was trapped inside an invisible container. Such an odd experience. Bumping into the walls didn't hurt. They were almost elastic. I could see through them, but no matter how hard I tried, I couldn't pass through them. This had never happened to me before. Not even dense boulders stopped me.

Then I saw a flash of light, coming from the far riverbank. I looked over to see a male torvee, standing on his back two legs and pointing something at me.

An alien! Like the one we saw enter the science building. Is this the same alien?

It was clear from the pressure on my back that the alien was drawing the container to him.

As I got closer I could see his eyes, flashing red, searching the container from top to bottom.

He seemed confused. His device showed he had captured something, but he could not see anything. I must have tripped some type of sensor, a very powerful sensor.

The container settled on the rocky bank. The alien clicked away on his device.

I sensed a draft come through the top of the container. He was opening it. I shot out of there as soon as I could.

I looked back to see the alien putting his hand inside and feeling all around. He never saw me.

Maybe he was trying to catch a bird to eat?

How interesting. But I cannot wait around to investigate. I am even further behind time-wise.

Forty-Two

Sonny

Leolie stood, took a step back, and studied Pidge.

"Think she'll make it through the portal tunnel?" I asked.

Leolie kept looking at Pidge, and sighed. "I do not see how. No way to breathe in there. The program creates a powerful vacuum. The gravitational pressures are crushing." She looked at me. "You remember."

I nodded. "Yeah. I thought I was being ripped apart, and I had to hold my breath for the entire trip."

Leolie looked back at Pidge. "You are young and strong. She is weak and soon will be old. Her arms will be whipped around and broken. She will not be able to hold her head up. Probably snap her neck. No way she would survive the tunnel." Large blue tears rolled down her green cheeks.

"But she will die if she stays here."

Leolie brushed away tears with her fingers. "So tell me my young problem solver, which is better?"

"She will die if she stays. But if she leaves, she at least has a chance, no matter how small."

"I told you. There is no way she can survive the journey."

"I could go with her. Hold her. Make sure her arms and head stay put."

Leolie stiffened. "All our scientists are gone. I need you here. Astrobia needs you here. And now, with Pidge gone, we need you even more."

"Please, Leolie. Let me go. ... Please."

"When I visited the palace, Doric told me all about his dungeons and told me that's where he puts people who defy him."

"Dungeons?"

"Yes, dungeons. Doric videoed-in just minutes ago. He is not happy about me crushing Sittu's listening device."

"He knows about that?"

"The Supreme Leader did not say so, but he wants to put Pidge in charge of Rynstat as soon as she is well."

"Does he know Pidge is an alien, and that she must have the enzyme to remain on Astrobia?"

"Of course not. He expects she will recover. I am only here now because Pidge is in such bad shape.

You know Doric and Sittu will be watching everything I do. I am sorry, Sonny, but I have no choice."

She turned and left the chamber.

Nooo. I want to go home. I have to go home. I melted to the floor, hitting Pidge on the shoulder as I did.

"Sonny," Pidge whispered.

I twisted to hear her.

Pidge looked straight ahead, her eyelids barely open. "Heard...you two. ... must not get Leolie...in trouble."

"But I—"

"Promise," Pidge interrupted. "Promise...you...will not go...with me."

I shook my head. "I can't."

"Then I...will not go. Neither will...Bennett."

Forty-Three

Breanne

I untangled myself from the two women and slowly stood up, rotating my arm to test my sore shoulder. But my shoulder was nothing compared to the pain these two must be feeling. They're too old to be diving on the floor and wrestling me. I watched Mrs. Pidgeon use a chair to drag herself up, then plop down on it, and lean back with her hand on her chest.

Oh, no. Not another heart attack. I watched her closely—face red, breathing hard. But she didn't seem to be in pain like before, and her breathing became more normal.

I looked back at Grams still sitting on the floor, staring, like she didn't know if she could get up. It had to have taken every ounce of her strength to tackle me and hang on for dear life while I struggled to get to the portal. She must be way more bruised up than I am. I hope she didn't break any bones.

I reached out both hands to help her up. As soon as she grabbed them we both sensed Sonny. I pulled her to her feet, and we kept holding hands.

Grams was a bit shaky, but her fingers were strong and her grip like a vice. "He's scared again," she said.

I nodded. "Scared but also...excited? ... Something about...Pidge. Yes, Pidge needs help."

"Pidge?" Mrs. Pidgeon snapped up straight. "Did you say Pidge? Needs help for what?"

"What about my Bennett?" Mrs. Turner asked.

I shrugged. "I don't know anymore about Pidge." I glanced up at the transom window where I thought Mrs. Turner was still watching the portal. "And we haven't sensed anything about Bennett."

Grams spoke up. "Memphis. He's thinking about Memphis."

Forty-Four

Bennett

I heard the light hum of one of the high-speed military transporters, and looked up just as it plowed into me. I found myself in the empty backseat, behind a young officer at the controls. I decided to stay put because he was headed in the direction of Rynstat at a speed well beyond my capacity.

I kept a watchful eye on the terrain, and bailed out near the observation complex. I sliced through the above-ground door and went directly to the portal chamber.

I found Pidge stretched out on the floor with her feet up, and Sonny sitting beside her staring at the floor. I hovered above her, checking her breathing.

Sonny! I'm back!

He looked up. "Bennett? Everything set?"

Yes. I looked at the digital clock on the computer screen. *Six minutes before the bomb goes off. Tell Leolie all is ready.*

Sonny moved slowly to tap the radio on Pidge's belt. "Leolie. Bennett's back," he said without emotion, as if his mind was elsewhere.

The radio clicked. "Be right there," Leolie said.

Seconds later Leolie came running in. "It is complete? The bomb is placed inside Lambou Mountain?"

"Bennett says it is done," Sonny said quietly, looking down.

Leolie seemed to freeze, staring at Pidge. "Any change?"

Sonny shook his head.

"Look, Sonny," Leolie said. "I have been thinking. The volcano will provide the diversion I need. And the only chance Pidge has of surviving the portal tunnel is if you protect her. I want you to go with Pidge."

Sonny practically jumped to his feet, like a jack in the box. "Really? You mean it? You want me to go?"

Leolie nodded. "To keep her safe."

"I will. I will. Thank you so much."

All of us are going home?

"Yes, Bennett. All three of us."

"Get yourselves ready," Leolie said. She held Pidge's feet while Sonny slid the stool away, then lowered her legs. She placed Pidge's injured arm across her chest, then placed the other arm on top of it. She gently stroked her cheek. "I think I like these freckles."

Leolie turned to Sonny. "You must wrap your arms around her and hold the back of her head close to you. That way you can protect her from the extreme forces of the vacuum."

Sonny nodded.

Sonny

Quickly now. Bennett thought. *Less than two minutes.*

"Bennett says it's time!" I announced.

Leolie gazed at Pidge. "Goodbye, my dear friend. I hope you make it to your home."

Leolie started for the door, turned and pointed to a large circular window on the ceiling.

"When I open the portal above you, Sonny, you will be jerked immediately into the tunnel. Hold on tightly, or Pidge will be yanked from your grasp. Then, at the other end, you have to hit the floor first because Pidge will have no strength to absorb the shock of landing."

Sonny nodded. "Thank you, Leolie."

Leolie ran from the chamber.

I am floating directly over you, Sonny. Bennett thought. *This will take every bit of strength you have. Do not let go of her. I will see you both in Memphis.*

I stretched out beside Pidge. Then I slid one arm under her, rolled her to me and cradled her head into my chest.

"I'm ready, Bennett."

I will be able to sense the explosion before you will. I will let you know. You will have only a second to take a deep breath before Leolie opens the portal.

I closed my eyes and concentrated with all my might to reach Breanne. *Bree! Coming through portal. We are all coming through the portal. Must catch Pidge.*

NOW! SONNY! DEEP BREATH!

I took a deep breath and pulled Pidge to me with all my might.

The portal snapped open with a roar of a tornado.

"Aaaah!"

The sudden jerk of the vacuum almost ripped Pidge away from me. I still had one hand behind her head and the other behind her back, but there was enough space between our bodies for a king size pillow.

We went head first into the tunnel and began tumbling. The pressures were greater than I remembered. I could feel her getting away from me.

My mind raced. *Don't let go! I promised to keep Pidge safe. I'm so weak. Pidge won't make it. It will be my fault. I'm such a wuss. Pull her back. Harder!*

But no matter how hard I tried, I couldn't bring her back into me. My muscles quivered. I felt my fingers losing their grip.

How much longer? I'm...losing...her...

That's when I read Bree's thoughts. *Hang on, Sonny. We'll catch you. We'll catch both of you. Just hang on.*

I tensed my whole body and pulled with everything I had.

Yes! I felt Pidge's head on my shoulder.

Just like my landing in Astrobia, our bodies rotated for our entry through the transom window feet first.

Forty-Five

Breanne

"Sonny's mood has changed," I said. "He's happy."

Grams reached for my hands. Her eyes lit up when we touched. "Yes, he's darn right excited."

"Now he's nervous."

"But not scared, just nervous. He's got somethin' to do. He's thinkin' about Memphis."

I sensed Sonny's thoughts getting louder. "No. Sonny's not just *thinking* about Memphis. He's *coming* to Memphis. Right now! He's got Pidge. Quick! Pull the mattresses over here. I'll move the ladder."

Grams and Mrs. Pidgeon dragged the mattresses to the door.

"He's coming," Mrs. Turner yelled. "My Bennett is coming. He's yelling to me, but I can't tell what he's saying over the wind."

We stood around the mattresses. The two women were wide-eyed, but only barely able to stand. Mrs. Pidgeon having had a heart attack after holding on to Sonny, and then holding me back from the portal. And tiny Grams, who just tackled me and held on with all her might, until she was exhausted.

No way they'd be able to catch two people dropping ten feet from the transom window. They'd be crushed. No. I've got to do this. I've got to catch them.

Our connection was getting stronger. I could read Sonny's mind without having to hold Grams' hand now.

How much longer? Sonny thought. *I'm...losing... her...*

I didn't know what 'I'm losing her' meant, but I knew Sonny needed help. He needed me. *Hang on, Sonny! We'll catch you. We'll catch both of you. Just hang on.*

I focused on the transom window.

"Oh, Bennett. You're home," I heard Mrs. Turner say.

Once again, my concentration was intense, putting everything in slow motion. I saw aqua boots inch their way through the window, followed by black dress shoes and white socks. Then legs and bodies. Sonny had his arms wrapped around someone...someone with greenish skin and red and purple hair. Pidge?

I jumped and tackled them both in midair. The tackle slowed their fall, and forced all three of us to land on the mattresses.

I don't know how long we stayed there before I opened my eyes. No idea where my glasses were. I glanced up to see the blurry outline of two women standing like mannequins—arms outstretched and frozen, mouths open wide. Sonny's thick black glasses hung from Grams' fingers.

I felt a crunch when I rolled back. I moved and felt around until I located my glasses. One arm had been broken off. I quickly stuck them on anyway, then looked down at the two arrivals. I could only see Sonny's back, as he lay on his side. Neither moved. I touched Sonny's shoulder. He moaned. I rolled him over, then stopped.

Beside him was the most bizarre creature I've ever seen. A young woman with spikes of purple hair poking through her red hair. Her skin looked like she had some disease—cream colored with pale green patches, all covered in freckles.

Grams dropped to her knees beside Sonny. "You came back! You're here! You okay, child? You hurt? Talk to me."

Sonny opened his eyes and blinked. Grams carefully placed his glasses on him, then helped him sit up.

He blinked some more, then reached out. "Grams? ... Grams! Oh, Grams. I'm home."

They wrapped their arms around each other, both crying softly.

On the other side of Sonny, I saw the green woman move her head ever so slightly.

Mrs. Pidgeon cautiously approached her. "Pidge? ... Is that you?" She lowered to one knee and studied the woman's face. A look of concern came over her face. "Dear Lord, what did they do to you?"

The green woman did not answer.

Grams pulled back from Sonny. "Let me look at you. You sure you're alright?"

Sonny took off his glasses and dried his eyes. "My arms feel like rubber. I don't think I'll be able to feed myself."

Grams smiled. "Don't you worry your head 'bout that, child. I'll feed you so's all you have to do is chew."

Sonny put his glasses back on and saw me. "Bree!" He reached out and I took his hand. "I read your mind." He turned. "You too, Grams. Wait a minute, how could I do that?"

I was smiling so big, my cheeks almost closed my eyes. "I'll explain it to you later."

We heard voices and looked up to see Bennett's and Mrs. Turner's spirits. She was looking him over from top to bottom. "I don't understand. How'd you get so old."

"Later, grandma," Bennett said. "I just want to be with you right now."

We watched them blend together in a loving embrace.

"Sonny?" Mrs. Pidgeon asked. "Is this my Pidge?"

"Sure is," Sonny said as he crawled on his hands and knees to the green woman. He touched Pidge's shoulder. "Pidge. It's Sonny. Can you hear me?"

Pidge moaned, barely opened her eyes.

Sonny looked back at me. "Can you get her some water?"

"In my desk drawer," Mrs. Pidgeon said.

I found an unopened water bottle and brought it back. When I got there, Mrs. Pidgeon was sitting on the mattress with Pidge's head in her lap. I twisted open the cap and handed her the bottle. She poured water into the cap and brought it to Pidge's lips.

Pidge licked her dry lips and took in the water. Her eyelids fluttered. "Aunt Marge?" she whispered.

"Yes, dear," Mrs. Pidgeon said. "I'm here. Would you like more water?"

Pidge gave the smallest of nods.

Mrs. Pidgeon raised her to a seated position and brought the bottle to her mouth. Pidge put a hand on top of her aunt's and took a sip. She took a few breaths before taking a bigger sip. She looked at her aunt, and then rested her head on Mrs. Pidgeon's shoulder.

"We made it, Pidge," Sonny said.

Pidge looked over. "What are you doing here?" she squeaked. "What about Leolie? You promised!"

Sonny shook his head. "I never promised not to leave Astrobia. Besides, it was Leolie's idea. She said the only chance you had of surviving the portal tunnel was if I went with you."

"She said that?" Pidge reached for another drink, and Mrs. Pidgeon brought the bottle to her lips.

Sonny waited for her to finish drinking. "Not only that, Leolie's the one who showed me how to hold on to you so the forces wouldn't break your arms, or break your neck."

"She did? And you held on to me? Through the entire tunnel?"

Sonny nodded. "And my friend Breanne over there kinda caught us when we came through the portal opening."

I gave her a little wave. "Hey, Pidge."

"Thanks, y'all," Pidge said, then looked at Sonny. "I owe you my life."

———◆———

"I'm fixin to do a Mickey D's run," Grams announced. "Anyone hungry?"

Sonny's hand shot up. "Me. All I had was one raw Astrobian vegetable. Tasted like an onion. Made my head buzz."

Pidge's voice was still weak. "Can't explain it, but I have a sudden craving for a Big Mac, fries and a *Coke*?"

"Your Earthly body is coming back quickly," Sonny said. "You think you can digest this kind of food after so many years of eating clean?"

"I can only tell you what I am dying to eat," Pidge said smiling. "And right now my stomach is craving some grease and fat and sugar."

"Okay, Sonny," Grams said. "Come with me. I'm not letting you outta my sight for a good long while. Come-on, Breanne. You can help carry stuff."

"I'm staying right here with Pidge," Mrs. Pidgeon said. "After we've eaten, y'all can explain what in the world happened to you."

Forty-Six

Sonny

Breanne called her mom to tell her she was eating a late lunch with me and Grams. We carried the food and drink back to the school library.

Pidge woofed down the Big Mac and fries. It perked her up quickly, and she physically changed right before our eyes. Within minutes almost all of the green skin faded away, and only a few lone purple spikes poked through her red hair. I think she even grew a few inches taller. She wasn't aging, but she didn't return to her thirteen-year old self either. Pidge was rapidly becoming a twenty-six-year old Earthling.

Breanne had a couple of fish sandwiches and a Doctor Pepper. Grams and Mrs. Pidgeon had salads and water. Me, I had a double order of chicken nuggets, fries and a strawberry shake.

Mrs. Pidgeon rapped her knuckles on one of the long tables. "Story time. Y'all gather 'round."

We all took a seat, leaving one end open for Bennett and his grandmother. I sat between Grams and Bree. Grams slipped her arm around mine and kept holding on. I explained to Pidge that when Breanne and I touched hands we could both see and hear ghosts.

"Even though we can't see him, Bennett can still hear what we're saying, right?" Pidge asked.

"That's right. So can his grandmother, Mrs. Turner. I nodded to the end of the table. "They're right next to one another, kinda sitting just above the table. Mrs. Turner says 'Hello.'"

Mrs. Pidgeon raised a hand. "Hello, Lorene. We have waited so long."

"You can see her, Aunt Marge?" Pidge asked.

Mrs. Pidgeon shook her head. "No, but we have been together since Bennett was taken, waiting for the two of you to come home."

I spoke up. "Bennett says it makes more sense for him to go first. I'll tell you what he's saying. Remember, Bennett's not the eighth grader he was when he was captured. Just being on the planet of Astrobia makes you age really fast. How long were you there, Bennett?"

"About four years as a living person," Bennett said. "Dying at the Earthly age of seventy-three. And I spent another ten years as a ghostly spirit, mostly trying to figure out how to get back to Memphis."

Mrs. Pidgeon gasped when I repeated Bennett's words.

Grams looked at me in disbelief.

I nodded. "I can tell you he was a brilliant scientist."

"I can attest to that," Pidge said.

Bennett smiled. "The Astrobians are mostly a peaceful people who are far more advanced than we are in science and medicine. They are particularly advanced in understanding the brain—especially the teenage brain. They use radio frequencies to hypnotize teens across the portal. I am sure Pidge and Sonny have no idea why they went to that transom window. I certainly do not."

I repeated Bennett's words, then added, "That's for sure."

Pidge shook her head. "I don't even remember doing it."

"Me neither," Breanne said.

"It all begins the instant you touch your finger to the transom window," Bennett said. "You are immediately sucked through the portal like you were on the scariest carnival ride ever. The G-forces are dangerously high, and the trip lasts about as long as you can hold your breath."

Pidge nodded. "And the landing isn't pretty either."

"I believe all of us landed at the feet of an Astrobian woman, right?" Bennett asked.

"Actually," I said. "My 'Astrobian woman' was Pidge."

Pidge laughed. "Yeah. And you were a mess. I thought you were going to barf on my shiny boots."

"For Pidge and me, the Astrobian woman was Zardina," Bennett said. "We learned so much from her. I was in my Earthly seventies when Zardina captured Pidge to be my replacement."

That's when Pidge jumped in. "Bennett died shortly after my arrival. I had already aged three Earth-years when Zardina discovered how to synthesize a special enzyme common to all Astrobians. As soon as she gave it to me, I stopped aging so rapidly and became an Astrobian."

I smiled. "She was the real deal. Scared me to death."

Pidge continued. "Zardina enrolled me as a six-teen-year old in their Science Academy. That's where I met Leolie. We have been great friends ever since."

"In her short time on Astrobia," Bennett said, "Pidge became one of the most respected scientists on the planet. You can be proud of her accomplishments, Mrs. Pidgeon."

"Thank you, Bennett," Pidge said. "That means a lot coming from you."

Mrs. Pidgeon smiled and took Pidge's hand.

Pidge patted her aunt's hand. "Four days ago there was a horrible accident. One of the planet's anti-matter generators blew up. Thousands of people were killed—my friends and co-workers, even our leader Zardina."

"Oh..." Mrs. Pidgeon said. "I'm so sorry."

Pidge made a tight-lipped smile, "It changed everything for me. I didn't get my enzyme injection and was quickly becoming an Earthling again. But that was not a good thing. I grew weak. I couldn't walk without help, and kept fainting. As soon as the enzyme completely left my body I would age a couple hundred Earth-years."

"And join me in the spirit world," Bennett said.

Pidge took a breath and let it out slowly. "And right in the middle of all of those problems Sonny showed up. He was only on Astrobia a few hours. But in that short time he was remarkable. He planned the diversion which allowed the three of us to escape. We could not have done it without Sonny."

"Come-on, Sonny," Breanne said. "Tell us about you."

"I've never been so scared," I said. "And I wouldn't have made it if you and Grams had not reached me."

"What do you mean, 'reached me?'" Pidge asked.

"Remember I told you that I could read Bennett's mind?"

Pidge nodded.

"Well, Breanne and I both read minds. And the two of us are especially good at reading each other's minds."

"Yes, but not across a half-billion light-years of space." Pidge said.

"I can't explain it."

Breanne leaned forward and looked at Grams on the other side of me. "We can. Can't we?"

Grams looked at Breanne. "Lord knows, I don't have a clue." Then she broke out in a big smile. "But we did it."

Grams high-fived Bree.

Breanne looked at me. "Turns out your Grams can read minds too. And her connection to you is very strong. When we held hands both of us could sense your feelings."

"You knew how scared I was?"

Breanne nodded.

I looked at one, then the other. "And that's when you made contact, telling me to 'think' and to 'get on with it?' "

"I was trying to help calm you down," Breanne said. "Grams was more kick-in-the-pants about you doing something."

Grams smiled.

Breanne looked at Pidge. "We knew how worried Sonny was about you, even though we had no idea what you were going through."

"I am in awe of your powers," Pidge said, then looked at me. "And I'm forever in your debt."

Mrs. Pidgeon gestured to Grams and Breanne. "I only caught snippets of their conversation about what they were sensing from Sonny. It scared me so that I kept the tin of nitroglycerin pills in my hand."

Pidge leaned over and hugged her aunt. She was definitely an Earthling again—a redheaded, freckle faced, hazel eyed Earthling. She still wore her Astrobian mid-calf aqua boots, beige shorts and beige pullover shirt with the gold scientific symbol in the upper right corner—a single cell with three orbiting electrons. Then, of course, there was the brightly colored chakata bird tattoo, now sprinkled with freckles.

Forty-Seven

Pidge

"Pidge?" Aunt Marge asked. "When was the last time you saw yourself in the mirror?"

"This morning when I brushed my teeth."

"Bet you won't recognize yourself now."

I looked at my arms and the back of my hands. "Geez. I haven't seen pink skin and freckles in over ten years. Where's a mirror?"

"Come with me," Aunt Marge said. "You, too, Breanne."

Aunt Marge led us down the hall and into the girls' restroom. She moved out of the way and left me staring into a full-length mirror at a woman I'd never seen before. A complete stranger, but she was wearing Astrobian clothes. I turned around to find her, but no one was there.

I turned back. There she was again.

I moved my arm. The stranger moved the same arm.

I touched my hair. The stranger touched her red hair. *That's really me. The last time I saw me with red hair I was a skinny thirteen-year-old with braces. Now I'm a twenty-six-year-old…woman.* I kept touching my face.

I tried to finger comb my hair, but it wouldn't stay put. "My hair's an absolute mess. Come to think of it, I haven't combed it since it turned purple."

"I think you're pretty, Pidge," Breanne said. "You could be a model."

I kept turning to see as much of me as I could.

"Breanne is right, Pidge," Aunt Marge said. "You are a beautiful young woman."

I felt my cheeks getting warm, and saw myself blush. And then I just started laughing and couldn't stop. Pretty soon Aunt Marge and Breanne were laughing too. Something I hadn't done in who-knows how long. It felt great.

As we calmed down, Aunt Marge said, "The others will be wondering what happened to us. We should go back. But before we go, take a good long look at your new self, Pidge."

I can't explain it, something had changed. I felt…at home.

We chatted on the way back to the library. Breanne and Aunt Marge returned to their seats, but I was too excited. So I began exploring the library.

I heard Grams. "Well? Tell us. What happened when Pidge looked in the mirror?"

"She didn't know her own self," Breanne said. "She actually turned around expecting to see a redheaded woman in an Astrobian outfit standing behind her."

Everyone laughed.

I saw a red book lying open on the floor. "What's this book doing on the floor?"

Aunt Marge pointed. "Don't touch that."

"That book looks familiar," Bennett said.

"Yeah," Sonny said. "Looks familiar to me, too.

"Me, three," I said, standing inches from it.

Breanne raised her hand. "Me, four. It's the last thing I remember before waking up on the floor."

"On the floor?" Sonny asked.

"Yup," Grams said. "She was on her way to that portal thing, up yonder. That's when I tackled her."

Sonny's eyes got big. "Tackled her? You tackled Bree?"

"You better believe it," Aunt Marge said. "What do the boys say? Oh, yeah. She took her out! Breanne still had that red book in her hands. I think it's the key to abducting our students."

"Bet you're right," I said. "Zardina designed the portals to identify students whose brain waves were similar to her own. Reading books about more advanced physics or astronomy activated those brain waves, and triggered the portals' attraction mechanism."

"Do you think that portal is open now?" Aunt Marge asked.

"Leolie is short two scientists— Sonny and me," I said. "I'm certain she opened that portal right after we passed through it."

"I sure don't wanna go back there," Bennett said.

Sonny shook his head. "Me neither, Bennett."

"I'd consider it," I said. "Of course, there's no synthesized W-35 enzyme, so I wouldn't last long."

Everyone looked at me.

"You're kidding, right?" Aunt Marge asked. "You just escaped. You could not possibly want to go back to that place."

"Actually, I wouldn't have left if I still had access to the enzyme. Never really had a friend when I was a student here. I was a real loner. Leolie is my first friend. Actually, she's my best friend in two worlds. I hated to leave her."

"You really do want to go back there, don't you?" Aunt Marge asked.

I walked back to the table and gave her a huge bear hug. "I thought about you every day, Aunt Marge. I truly love you."

"Same here. I thought about you every day as well. And I so dearly love you."

I pulled back. "No sense talking about it. I'm not going anywhere without the enzyme."

Sonny spoke up. "Wait a minute." He grabbed Breanne's hand so they could see and hear him. "Bennett says he has a confession."

All eyes turned to Bennett's end of the table.

"I desperately wanted to leave Astrobia," Bennett said. "I'd tried several times to break through the transom portal, but it was always closed. I couldn't get through even in my ghostly form. I thought I'd be in Astrobia forever. But everything changed when you missed your enzyme injection, Pidge."

Sonny held up a hand for Bennett to stop, so he could repeat his words.

"Then a few days later the anti-matter explosion destroyed any record of how Zardina created the enzyme. Your only chance for survival, Pidge, was to return to Earth. And even though the Supreme Leader ordered Leolie not to open the portal, she was going to do it for her best friend."

Sonny repeated what Bennett had said. Breanne helped with a few things he forgot. He motioned for Bennett to continue.

"So, for the first time since my arrival on Astrobia, almost thirteen years ago, there was a chance. A chance that the portal would be open. A chance for me to get back to Memphis. That is why I agreed to follow every harebrained idea Sonny had, even when I thought he was off his rocker."

Everyone laughed when Sonny repeated Bennett's words, even Sonny.

"There were a whole lot of things that had to fall into place to make my dream become reality and open the portal to earth. It was never easy. On top of all of that, Pidge refused to leave Astrobia if Leolie would get in trouble for disobeying an order."

Again, Sonny repeated Bennett's words.

"We were at a standstill until Sonny dreamed up a brilliant plan to set off a volcanic eruption as a diversion, so the authorities would not be able to tell if any beings were passing through the open portal."

I spoke up. "I agree with everything you've said, Bennett. In fact, I made the bomb that you carried to the volcano that set off the eruption so we could leave undetected. So I don't understand what you are confessing."

"Yes. But I knew something neither you nor Leolie did."

"What?" I asked. "What did you know?"

"As a ghost I spent years hanging around Zardina. I knew everything she did. I knew where the enzyme formula was hidden."

"But it was all destroyed in the blast."

"That's just it," Bennett said. "About a year ago, Zardina hid a copy of the formula at Rynstat inside the portal chamber, along with several automatic-injector syringes filled with the prepared enzyme. Of course, as a ghost, I had no way to tell anyone. That is until Sonny arrived, and he could read my mind. So I made sure I never thought about it, when I was around Sonny."

I raised up off my chair. "What? You knew where a supply of the enzyme was and you let me almost die?"

"Not completely correct, Pidge," Bennett said. "It was essential that you live so my plan would work. I had watched Zardina carefully test her prepared enzyme. I knew exactly how long it would last in your body. I kept a close eye on you all the time."

I stared at the tabletop feeling my neck growing warm. The heat moved up to my face, like I was catching fire.

"Pidge, if you knew, you would have used the enzyme and stayed on Astrobia. Then there would be no reason for Leolie to open the portal, and I would still be stuck on that planet. And so would Sonny. And you would never have seen your aunt again."

No one said a word.

I couldn't sort out my feelings. I was furious with Bennett for not telling me about the enzyme. At the same time, I was grateful for having been able to return to Earth—to see my aunt, to see my grownup Earthling self. But I miss Leolie. And the pain of losing Zardina and my colleagues breaks my Earthly heart just as it did my Astrobian heart.

"I realize how selfish this sounds, Pidge," Bennett said. "But if you were in my place, what would you have done?"

The question stunned me. *What would I have done?*

I felt Aunt Marge's gentle hand on my back. She leaned into me and spoke softly. "Sounds like a fair question, Pidge. You, more than any other person, know what Bennett has been through. He didn't have a friend like you did. No reason for him to stay. So? ... What would you have done in his place?"

Bennett's question forced me into my head, away from my feelings. My face cooled as I logically considered his situation. ... *He really had no options. I would have done the same thing.*

Forty-Eight

Breanne

I looked around the table. Grams still had her arm slipped inside Sonny's arm. They were leaning on each other, their eyes closed. Mrs. Pidgeon slouched back in her chair, staring somewhere over the middle of the table.

I wasn't doing much better. I had all I could do to keep my eyes open. I rotated my shoulder to get the crick out of it.

We all were exhausted. That is, everyone except Pidge. She explored the library shelves, practically beaming with energy.

I think I'll get the Big Mac next time.

Pidge came around the end of the third row and saw me watching her. She put her finger to her lips, then motioned for me to follow as she walked away.

I eased quietly from my chair and joined her in the far corner of the room.

Pidge spoke softly. "Aunt Marge told me how you saved her life when she was having heart problems. I am so grateful." She reached up and hugged me.

"I just did what Mrs. Turner and your aunt told me to do."

"Mrs. Turner?"

"Yeah. She's the one who yelled for me to help. I can't see ghosts without touching Sonny, but I can hear them just fine."

"Amazing."

"I think you're amazing," I said. "You must know so much stuff about science that no one on earth knows."

Pidge smiled. "It's true. I've learned a few things."

"You could join NASA and help the space program."

"I probably could. But I've been thinking." She looked over at Mrs. Pidgeon. "There are so few scientists left on Astrobia after that horrible explosion. And Leolie's now the new Science Commander."

"I don't understand."

"My friend Leolie needs my help, and I want to help her."

I nodded slowly, as if I kinda knew what she was saying but afraid of where the conversation was going. My head stopped moving. "But you just got here. And what about your aunt? She's waited so long for you to come back."

"I know. I don't want to hurt her. But I don't want to hurt Leolie either. I don't know what to do."

I didn't know what to say.

Pidge paused. "Remember? Bennett asked me what I'd do if I were in his place?"

"I remember," I said. "He wanted to return to earth so badly that he let you get real sick. It almost killed you."

"Right. And when I used my logical scientific brain, the one the Astrobians developed, I understood why Bennett did it. And yes, if I was back on Astrobia, I probably would have done the same thing he did."

"But you're on earth now."

"Exactly. My Astrobian brain cell connections are sitting right beside my Earthly brain cell connections. And my Earthly brain is more emotional. That makes it impossible for me to make a decision based only on logic."

"I don't get it."

"Look. On Earth I remember hearing grownups say, 'fish gotta swim, birds gotta fly and people gotta feel.' Feelings are very important. But on Astrobia they would say, 'fish gotta swim, birds gotta fly, and people gotta think.' "

"You mean Astrobians don't have any feelings?"

"Oh, they have feelings, but they rarely show them. On Astrobia, logic is considered a strength and emotion is considered a weakness."

"Like some of the kids at school. Always acting tough, like nothing bothers them."

Pidge shook her head. "That's not logic. Solving problems with logic is based on facts, or perceived facts. Like, 'if box A contains two white baseballs and box C contains one orange baseball, then box A must weigh more than box C.' This logical conclusion is something almost everyone can agree on because the color of the baseball makes no difference in its weight."

"Okay..."

"But if you used emotion to solve problems, you might mistakenly conclude that box C is larger because you grew up watching Sesame Street and learned that 'C' stands for 'cookie.' Because the thought of cookies makes you happy, you choose box C."

I had to laugh. "Sounds like something Cookie Monster would do."

"Making decisions based on emotion is highly personal, and not always a good way to solve problems—scientific or personal. We all get sad, or scared, or worried. The difference is many kids are taught it's okay to show only one negative emotion—anger. So that's what they do, even when they're actually scared."

"Like bullies?"

"Yeah, especially bullies do that. The more afraid they are, the more they act angry to cover it up."

"Did you learn all this on Astrobia?"

Pidge shook her head. "Actually, I never even thought about it until today, here on Earth."

"Today?"

"Yeah. When Bennett asked me that question. I found myself bouncing from the Astrobian part of my brain to the Earthly part of my brain. It made me intensely aware of the differences."

"Is your Astrobian brain super logical?"

"Yeah. The W-35 enzyme gave me all the physical characteristics of an Astrobian—I looked like them and I thought like them. But I always had enough Earthling qualities in me to have emotions, and sometimes even show my feelings. I think that's why Leolie and I are such close friends, like you and Sonny. ... So, Breanne? What would you do if Sonny was all alone on Astrobia and needed you?"

I stepped back, not sure what to say.

Pidge open her hands in front of her. "You just went through this yourself. And from what I heard, you were on your way to Astrobia when Sonny's grandmother tackled you and Aunt Marge held you down till you came to your senses."

"I didn't do it on purpose. At least, I don't think I did. Maybe I gave off the right signals for the portal beam to kick in. But I didn't just decide to do it."

"However it happened, it wasn't a logical decision. It was an emotional one. You wanted to help your friend, right?"

"Of course. He's my friend."

"You were prepared to make a big sacrifice," Pidge said. "Even bigger since you knew about how Bennett aged."

"I wasn't thinking about that..."

"That's clear. I mean the part about not thinking with your logical brain."

"She's only a child, Pidge," Mrs. Pidgeon said.

We both jumped and looked back.

Mrs. Pidgeon stood right behind us. She moved closer and put an arm around both of us. "That's the difference, Pidge. You, on the other hand are an adult now. An adult with life experiences we will never have. It sounds as if you are struggling with this decision."

"You and I have just gotten back together after ten years, Aunt Marge. I..."

Mrs. Pidgeon let go of me and put Pidge in a bear hug. I heard her whisper. "Because I love you, I would never stand in the way of you doing what makes you happy." She pulled back. "Parents have been saying goodbye to their children for as long as we have been on this Earth. You might go off to college, or get married, go on a dangerous hunting trip, or travel overseas ... or even go to another planet. As long as it is what you want to do, I will stand behind you."

Pidge kinda froze for a few seconds before speaking. "Really? I mean, really, you understand?"

Mrs. Pidgeon nodded. "It doesn't mean I won't miss you terribly. And certainly doesn't mean I won't be worried about you. But, yes. I understand."

Mrs. Pidgeon turned and looked up at me. "If Pidge were your age, I would be too frightened to let her go. So, do me and your parents a favor, Breanne. Don't leave Earth until you are older. Much older."

I shook my head. "No, ma'am."

"And, Breanne...?"

"Ma'am?"

"Sonny is very lucky to have a friend like you."

Forty-Nine

Sonny

Mrs. Pidgeon, Pidge and Breanne came back to the table. Bree sat next to me. "Take my hand, Sonny. I've got a feeling Bennett and Mrs. Turner will be leaving us very soon."

I reached over and grabbed her hand. We found the two spirits suspended near the front wall, close together and smiling. As old as Bennett was, the two looked more like brother and sister instead of grandson and grandmother. I motioned for them to join us at the table.

Breanne whispered to me. "How about I say what Mrs. Turner says, and you do the same for Bennett?"

I nodded. "Good idea."

The two spirits floated over and hovered above the end of the table.

Breanne turned in her chair to look at the spirits. "We were wondering if you might be getting ready to cross over, now that you are back together."

Mrs. Turner smiled. "Oh, yes, sweet child. I am definitely ready."

Bennett waited for Breanne to tell the others what his grandmother said. "Same for me," he said. "The pull has been getting stronger by the minute. It won't be long now."

I repeated Bennett's words.

Mrs. Pidgeon looked surprised. "I didn't realize they'd be leaving so soon."

"We have both hung around for a long time, waiting for things to be right," Mrs. Turner said. "Waiting for my Bennett to come home."

Tears welled up in Mrs. Pidgeon's eyes. "I'm so grateful for your friendship all these years, Lorene. I never would have made it without you."

Mrs. Turner floated to her friend and placed a hand on her shoulder.

Mrs. Pidgeon sat back quickly, glanced at her shoulder, then looked at Breanne.

Breanne smiled and nodded. "Mrs. Turner is right beside you. Her hand is on your shoulder."

Mrs. Pidgeon raised a hand to her shoulder and leaned her head as if to cuddle with her friend.

"The feeling is mutual, Marge," Mrs. Turner said. "And I am so happy Pidge has returned to you."

No one spoke for several seconds.

Bennett broke the silence. "I am glad to see how well you have recovered, Pidge. I am sorry for making you go through all the pain of becoming human again. Please forgive me."

"Nothing to forgive, Bennett. Like you said, I never would have seen my Aunt Marge if you had told me about the hidden enzyme. I'm glad you did what you did. Thank you."

"We could not help but overhear your discussion about returning to Astrobia," Bennett said. "Have you decided yet?"

Pidge looked at her aunt and took her hand. "Yes. I have decided to return. I owe it to Leolie."

"I thought you might do that," Bennett said. "I would be remiss if I did not tell you a few things that you may find helpful."

I spent the next ten minutes repeating Bennett's words about Zardina, Doric, and his concern that aliens had been entering and leaving Astrobia at will.

"Thank you, Bennett," Pidge said. "I will share your information with Leolie."

Mrs. Turner floated up. "It is time, dear friends. We are being called."

Bennett joined her, and they hung just under the ceiling. "Goodbye and good luck to you all," he said. "Especially to you, Pidge."

Mrs. Turner raised her hand in a goodbye. "We will be waiting for you on the other side."

Breanne and I watched as they disappeared through the ceiling.

Fifty

Pidge

My mind raced. *How do I say goodbye? Why is it so easy to return to Astrobia, but so hard to leave Earth? ... I don't think Sonny's grandmother has let go of him since we arrived. And Breanne hasn't strayed from his side either. I'm no different. I'm still holding on to Aunt Marge's hand. Family. Friends. Such powerful bonds. We can't live without them...at least on Earth.*

But even on Astrobia where such relationships are not as common, I have a friend with whom I share a powerful bond—Leolie. I must go back.

Aunt Marge put her arm around me. "Penny for your thoughts."

I looked into her eyes. "It's time."

Aunt Marge forced a small smile. "I know." She pulled me into a warm embrace.

When we eased back, I couldn't focus on her face. My tears blurred everything.

Aunt Marge kissed my cheek and looked across the table. "Pidge is leaving now," she said softly.

Grams perked up. "Leaving? Now?"

"She wants to return to her friend on Astrobia."

"Leolie?" Sonny asked.

I nodded. "I will try to keep in touch." I pulled the small two-way radio off my belt and slid it across the table to Sonny.

"Whoa!" he said. "This is so cool." He bounced it in his hand. "I used this once to call Leolie."

"You did? The radio on my belt? I don't remember that."

"You were kinda out of it. I'd seen you use your radio before. So, when Bennett came back from putting the bomb in the volcano, I called Leolie to tell her everything was ready."

Sonny turned and passed the radio to Breanne. "Check this out, Bree. Feel how light it is. It must be made from one of Astrobia's prized elements."

I smiled. "Good logical analysis, Sonny."

Breanne took it. "Kinda looks like a tiny doorbell." She looked up at me. "Does it work now?"

I shook my head. "The old radio frequencies used to create this portal are interfering with the signal. It's remarkable that you and Grams could communicate through this portal with your minds better than I can with this high-tech device."

Breanne leaned back and high-fived Grams behind Sonny.

I pointed. "Leolie will be reprogramming all the portals using radio frequencies that match the technology of this radio. Once she does that I will try to contact you."

"Really?" Sonny said. "You think you can do that?"

"I'm going to try. Leave the radio here in the library, in line with the portal. I'll send a non-voice signal first to alert you. If you hear the ping, just tap the radio once and I'll know you received the signal. Tap the radio twice when no one else is around, and I'll talk to you."

Breanne slid the radio to Aunt Marge.

I stood up and took a deep breath. "You three keep taking care of each other," I said to Breanne, Sonny and Grams. Then I hugged Aunt Marge. "I love you."

"And I so love you, sweet Pidge," Aunt Marge said. "You be careful out there."

"Please don't worry. I'll be fine."

Sonny and Breanne pulled the ladder over and positioned it under the transom window.

I climbed up, gave one last wave goodbye, and squared up to face the window. Instantly, a flashback overwhelmed me.

PANIC ATTACK!

It was like I was thirteen. Being sucked into the portal for the first time.

Goose bumps covered my body and my red hair sprang up on the back of my neck.

My vision blurred.

My ears rang with an odd echo, like I was in a deep cave.

I lost my balance and reached out. My hand slapped against the wall, beside the window.

I heard Breanne's sharp voice in the distance. "Pidge! You all right?"

Then Sonny's command. "Deep breath!"

I obeyed—filled my lungs and slowly exhaled. The fear gradually faded away, like a wave washing down from my hair to my toes. I steadied myself against the wall until my head cleared and my balance returned. I blew out a breath.

"Pidge!" Breanne said. "What happened?"

I looked down at my new friends. "Panic attack. ... For a second I was back in the eighth grade again, going through the portal, and scared to death. Thought I'd forgotten all that. Guess not. ... I'm better now."

"Did it twice today," Sonny said. "The portal's so powerful. Harder than I could imagine. Didn't think I'd make it either time. But then it was over."

I nodded. "I've done it twice, as well. But I only remember the first time."

Fifty-One

Leolie

The blinking cursor sat over the 'go' button on the rewritten portal program. Lambou Mountain filled the wall screen. Three, two, one…

I watched debris fly from the crater. Seconds later the eruption came, blowing off more of the mountain top.

"Ellie!" I said. "Open the Astrobian portal to Earth."

"Yes, Leolie."

One second later I saw a disturbance in the electro-magnetic field sensor on my computer.

Pidge is gone. Pidge is … gone.

I watched the field sensor's line flatten out. On the wall screen, a massive cloud of dark smoke billowed out from the mountain. Lava spilled down one side of the mountain.

It is done. Pidge has entered the Earth portal. Did I do the right thing letting Sonny go with her? He's just a kid. Should I have trusted him? Is Pidge alive?

"Ellie, close the Astrobian portal to Earth, and open the Earth portal to Astrobia."

"Yes, Leolie."

I sat back, my hands dropped onto my lap.

Suddenly the screen filled with Sittu's face. "What just happened, Science Commander?"

Did he see the jump on the electro-magnetic field sensor? Quick. Talk about the volcano. "A volcano erupted," I said. "Did you not receive word? Lambou Mountain, up in the northern sector. Readouts show limited power on the explosivity indicator. No population centers or energy stations nearby, so no loss of life or damage."

"I know all that," Sittu said. "I want to know why you failed the Supreme Leader."

Oh, no. He did see the electro-magnetic disturbance. "Failed?"

"You know good and well that your observation complex is supposed to predict these eruptions. How did you miss this one?"

No. He did not see it. "If you will check the probability log you will see that Lambou Mountain had a ninety-seven percent chance of erupting within the next two years," I said. "Today is clearly within the 'next two year' period."

"Surely you can do better than that, Science Commander. I need to know when a volcano will erupt."

"<u>You</u> need to know?"

"Some fool programmed our computers to jump instantly to view any volcanic eruption," Sittu said.

"You are well aware Zardina wrote that program years ago, after volcanic eruptions killed so many citizens. That way, everyone at the Palace would be immediately alerted to any new catastrophe."

"Yes," Sittu said. "But I was involved in Palace business when the alert broke my connection."

"You mean you were spying on me when you lost the connection. Just like you 'lost the connection' when I crushed the data collection device you hid under my console."

Sittu said nothing.

"Never do anything like that again," I said forcefully.

Still Sittu said nothing.

I continued to be forceful. "I expect the Supreme Leader is anxiously awaiting your report about the eruption, Sittu. You better attend to that right now. And you have my permission to tell him you got the report from me. Leolie, signing off!"

It worked. ... Sonny's plan. Pidge's bomb. And Bennett's delivery. The diversion worked perfectly. Brilliantly executed. ... But now they are all gone.

I went to the dining chamber to get something to eat. I felt so alone. Too alone to have an appetite.

"Ellie, display the parallel universes."

"Yes, Leolie."

The screen lit up.

"Highlight Earth."

"Would you like to choose a color?"

"Yes I would. Make it pink with tiny red spots."

"As you wish, Leolie."

Earth stood out from the other planets. *I hope you are well, Pidge.*

I sipped a cup of tea and watched the screen for a long time before I returned to the observation chamber to monitor the eruption. No sooner than I sat down, the electro-magnetic field sensor rapidly zigzagged across the screen.

"Whoa!" *The Earth portal is open. I must have captured an Earthling. I hope she or he is as smart as Pidge or Sonny.*

I ran to the portal chamber to find a life form squatting on the floor, facing away from me and breathing hard. But something did not make sense. This alien wore Astrobian boots.

The alien slowly stood. *Astrobia clothes? Bushy red hair?*

It turned around. *A female.*

The alien raised a hand. "Hi, Leolie."

I stepped back. "Huh? How do you know my name?"

"It's me. Pidge."

Pidge? "How do you know Pidge?"

The alien opened her arms and slowly turned around so I could get a good look. "This is how I appear in my Earthly body."

"Pidge! Is it really you?"

We both moved forward and embraced.

I pulled back, held her at arm's length and looked her over carefully. She was taller. Blue-green eyes with a white sclera. Cream-color skin. Red hair. Freckles everywhere. I peppered her with questions without waiting for her to answer. "What happened to you? Are you well? How old are you? Why are you here? Did you forget there is no enzyme?"

Pidge said nothing. She smiled and guided me across the room. "It's been a really long day for both of us, Leolie. How about we sit down and talk?"

Fifty-Two

Breanne

"Bye, Pidge," Sonny and I said as she held her hands up to the transom window for the second time. She gave us a final look and pushed through.

The last thing we saw were Pidge's boots disappearing into the portal.

We kept staring up at the window. Neither of us spoke for a good minute before Sonny said, "Guess we can put the ladder back where we found it. It'll be easier if we just pull it."

I nodded.

The ladder made a soft scraping sound on the wooden floor as we dragged it to the back of the library. When we stopped, I heard sniffling and turned to see Mrs. Pidgeon dab her eyes with a tissue. Grams sat beside her gently patting her hand.

"Gotta be hard to say goodbye," I said. "Glad you're not going back there, Sonny."

Sonny's whole body shivered. "Me, too. Nobody was mean to me. ... Well, they did lock me up in that shoe-box of a closet—twice. But even then they were nice about it."

I glanced at the transom window. "Pidge must really like Leolie to go back there."

"Yeah," Sonny said. "The two of them got along real well. Course, Pidge just got sicker and sicker. Leolie was really worried."

I sat on the second step of the ladder. "What's Leolie look like?"

"Look like?" Sonny appeared to be searching his memory. "Let's see. Bright green skin, brown eyes with yellow sclera, spiked purple hair, and just a bit taller than me."

"Did Pidge look like that?"

He nodded and pointed to his upper arm. "Except she had that bird tattoo right here. Pidge is the one who pulled me off the floor when I crash-landed from the portal. Then Leolie came in. If Pidge hadn't started changing back to her Earthly self, I'd probably still be trying to tell the two of them apart."

"Was Leolie nice?"

Sonny shrugged. "I wouldn't call Leolie nice. All business. More like a little general, barking orders.

Well, at least to me. Not someone I'd want to be in the same car with on a long trip."

"You wouldn't want to be in a car with anybody on a long trip, Sonny Elliott."

"Probably not."

"Hey, Sonny?"

"Yeah?"

"You don't have to worry about telling your Grams what happened today because she already knows. But my parents don't know anything. What am I gonna say?"

"You think they'd believe you if you told 'em?"

I shook my head.

"What if Grams told them?" he asked.

"That's a great idea. Think she'd do it?"

"Don't know. You can ask her."

I followed Sonny back to the table.

Grams had been watching us as we walked back. "Looks like you two been chewin' on somethin'," she said. "Come on. Spit it out."

Sonny gestured to me. "She's got a problem, Grams. Go ahead, Bree. Ask her."

I gave Sonny a disapproving look, then turned to Grams. "I think I should tell my parents about today. But I don't know what to say."

Mrs. Pidgeon spoke up. "Please, don't say anything. There's no way it wouldn't get out. It will only spell trouble for me. And like before, when talk of alternate worlds and portals gets out, no one will believe it. They'll come after me thinking I'm off my rocker. This time I'd lose my job. And if I lose my job I won't be here to receive Pidge's call."

"But I have to tell them something," I said. "And I can't lie to them."

Grams gestured to the transom window. "Tell them the part that's not about that," Grams said. "They won't be surprised that you talked to ghosts. So tell them you met Mrs. Turner and her grandson Bennett."

Mrs. Pidgeon nodded. "Yes. That would be okay. Promise me you won't tell anyone about the portal. Please, Breanne."

Fifty-Three

Pidge

I led Leolie across the portal chamber to a small round table. We sat in metal chairs, facing one another. She stared at me.

I smiled. "I promise. It's me. ... Take a good look. I'll soon return to my Astrobian self."

"What? Return to your Astrobian self? How?"

I left the table and walked to the right side of the door. I slid my hand over the wall until I felt the slight indentation, then pushed. A panel moved back and slid sideways revealing a small hiding place. I took out an automatic-injector syringe and returned to the table.

Leolie's mouth dropped open. "Is that what I think it is?"

I nodded. "The W-35 enzyme. The formula is there, as well."

I held the syringe upright, then punched the bottom of it into my thigh. The needle automatically popped out, stuck me, and injected the correct amount of the enzyme. "We'll see how long before I become my Astrobian self again."

Leolie was still wide-eyed. "I do not understand. Who hid the enzyme?"

"Zardina."

"How did you find out about it?"

"Bennett."

"Bennett? He made it through the portal, too? But how could he tell you? ... Oh. Sonny read his mind."

"Right. Actually, Sonny and his friend Breanne. Through them, Bennett told me Zardina hid a copy of the formula and a supply of the enzyme here at Rynstat in case new aliens were captured."

Leolie pointed. "The last time I saw you, you were lying unconscious on this very floor. Your green skin had turned a cream color, freckles popped out all over, and little of your purple hair remained. You would not have survived on Astrobia another hour. I did not think you would survive the portal either. But if there was even the slightest chance, I had to try."

"I'm so grateful you did."

"I positioned you in Sonny's grasp to protect your arms and head. Then I went to the observation chamber to wait for the bomb to go off. It exploded precisely at Two-fifteen triggering Lambou Mountain's eruption.

That's when I opened the portal, and you were sucked inside. Tell me what happened after that, Pidge. I want to hear every detail."

I told Leolie about my trip to Earth—Sonny protecting me in the portal, waking up on a mattress in the school library, being with my Aunt Marge, and about Sonny's grandmother and friend being able to tele-pathically communicate with him while he was here on Astrobia.

I told her about my bi-world experience of dealing with the logical and emotional sides of me. How that led me to realize the importance of friendship and led to my decision to return to my good friend on Astrobia.

"From the beginning, you were different from other students at the Science Academy, Pidge. Now, from what you have told me, I can see it was the emotional part of you that was unique. I think it is what made it easy to be your friend. I like that part of you."

I started to tell Leolie about my conversations with Bennett, but I felt woozy as the enzyme took effect.

Leolie pointed. "Your skin is starting to glow."

"I think I need to lie down for a while."

Leolie walked me to my sleep chamber. Before lying down I took a long look in the mirror. I wanted to remember me as an adult Earthling.

Fifty-Four

Leolie

I waited until Pidge sat on the bed, pulled off her boots and collapsed onto the pillow before I left for the observation chamber.

Something was different. The complex seemed brighter. The air smelled fresher. My boot steps sounded crisper and stronger. I was different. I held my shoulders back, my chin up. My face felt odd...a smile? And I felt weird. I felt...happy. Pidge survived. She came back. My friend came back and I was experiencing positive emotions.

In the observation chamber I pulled up a view of Lambou Mountain. A massive gray cloud of ash drifted from the mountain. Red hot lava flowed slowly down the south side and created a fiery path into the forest. Clouds of steam rose from the lava and blocked my line of sight to the mountain top.

"Ellie. Provide additional views of Lambou Mountain."

"Additional views provided, Leolie."

Less steam covered the north side, and it appeared that a large portion of the crater wall was missing.

The east view showed transporters. I noted two on the ground and three airborne. Investigators. The largest transporter bore the Palace seal—Doric. The Supreme Leader was personally inspecting the damage.

I experienced another emotion—worry. *What will the investigators find?* Any physical evidence of Pidge's bomb should have been incinerated by the lava. And detection of the trace odors of the explosive should be hidden by the volcano's release of potent sulfur dioxide gas.

Several hours later I heard the whoosh of the entrance door. I tapped the internal cameras and watched as Sittu entered Rynstat.

What is he doing here?...Pidge?...Pidge! He cannot see her. Not yet.

Sittu strode into the observation chamber.

I kept looking at the wall screen.

"Well, Science Commander. I see you know our Supreme Leader is inspecting the damage caused by Lambou Mountain's unexpected eruption. He is quite disturbed by this and insisted on leading an investigation."

"Greetings to you, too, Sittu. What is the purpose of your unannounced visit?"

"The Supreme Leader ordered me to check on the status of Officer Pidge's health. I brought along a hazardous materials gas mask for my own protection."

"I have told you that she is having a reaction to the chemicals and gases released by the explosion at Bannar. She is not contagious. You do not need a hazmat mask."

"So you said."

"Pidge is doing better, but she is sleeping and cannot be disturbed."

"I will only look in from the doorway. I have no intention of getting closer than that anyway."

"But merely opening the door will disturb her."

"I must insist, Science Commander. I have my orders."

I sighed. "She is in her sleep chamber."

Sittu stepped to the side and gestured for me to go first. "You will need to take me to her."

I walked slowly as Sittu followed.

When we arrived at Pidge's sleep chamber, Sittu said, "Wait. I need to put on my protective mask."

I held back, glad for even a few more seconds. Precious time for the enzyme to keep working.

Sittu looked like a frightened child as he struggled into his hazmat mask. "Okay," he announced, his voice muted by the mask, as if he were speaking through a thick blanket. "Open the door."

Whoosh.

I held my breath.

Sittu stepped forward. "I don't believe it."

I peeked in. Spiked purple hair overwhelmed strands of red. Green skin covered her arms, legs and face. It was only pale green, but there were no blotches. Pidge did, however, still have her freckles.

Sittu practically jumped into the hallway and tore off his mask. "What kind of magic have you done? This is not the same person."

"No magic, Sittu. Only my special soup made from hydroponic vegetables."

Sittu wheeled around and strode down the hall. I heard the double whoosh of the entrance door. I looked back at Pidge, still peacefully asleep. My smile came back.

Fifty-Five

Pidge

The next thing I remember, the door whooshed open. I looked up, blurry eyed, to see Leolie carrying a tray of fruits and vegetables, the same kind I had brought to Sonny. But unlike his reaction, my mouth watered. I sat up, hungry.

Leolie smiled broadly. "My Astrobian Pidge is back."

"Huh?"

She motioned with her head. "See for yourself."

I rolled out of bed and padded barefoot over to the mirror. What a surprise. Bright green skin, spiked purple hair, large brown eyes surrounded by glowing yellow, and a freckle-less chakata bird tattoo. Staring back at me was indeed, the Astrobian Pidge.

"Welcome back," Leolie said, setting the tray on the table. "Here is something to nourish your new body."

"It looks wonderful."

"When you are finished eating you can find me in the observation chamber," Leolie said as she left.

I could not believe it. The Astrobian veggies and fruits tasted as good as the Big Mac and fries tasted back on Earth. The coconut water tasted wonderful, and the smell reminded me of my favorite waterfall. I consumed everything and went looking for Leolie.

I found her standing in front of the observation chamber's wall screen, studying Lambou Mountain.

Leolie smiled. "You slept for almost twenty hours. I do not know your sleeping habits on Earth, but on Astrobia that is way longer than usual. How are you feeling?"

I moved my arms and legs. "Good. Surprisingly good. And, no. We Earthlings usually sleep seven or eight hours. About the same as here. I think my body was busy becoming Astrobian."

Leolie laughed.

"Heard any more from Doric about the volcano?"

"No. But we did get a video call from Sittu right after you and Sonny entered the portal for earth."

"Did he detect us leaving?"

"I was afraid he did," Leolie said. "But it turned out he was upset because the eruption automatically triggered his computers to switch to Lambou Mountain. He said because of the switch, he could not do his job."

"His job?"

"Yes. Spying on everyone. More specifically, spying on me."

"Did you tell him off?"

Leolie nodded. "I told him never to plant any bugs at Rynstat again."

"What did he say?"

"Nothing."

"Okay...," I said. "You think he will stop?"

"I am not certain he can stop. It is what he is good at."

"Did he ask about me?"

"Not then. But he showed up here about ten hours ago to see you."

"Me? Why me?"

"Said Doric ordered him to check your health status."

Panic overcame me. Thoughts ricocheted inside my head and questions gushed from my mouth without waiting for answers. "What did you do?" "Did Sittu come to my sleep chamber?" "What did he see?" "Why is Doric concerned about _my_ health?"

Leolie gestured with both hands for me to calm down. "I had no choice. I took Sittu to your sleep chamber. He was so scared he wore a hazmat mask."

"What?"

"He was convinced you were contagious."

"Oh..."

"Your color had mostly returned." Leolie smiled. "But you still had your freckles."

I looked at my arms—no sign of freckles.

"Sittu could not believe your improvement. He accused me of using some kind of cosmic magic, then left."

"Oh, Leolie. What would have happened to you if I had not returned to Astrobia? If Sittu had come to see me while I was on earth?"

"I do not want to think about it."

"Do you think Doric really sent Sittu to check on me?"

Leolie nodded. "Remember? Sittu saw you when he came here to plant that data-collection device."

"I remember."

"After receiving Sittu's report, Doric videoed in to ask about you. The Supreme Leader was very concerned. By then you had gotten much worse. You were barely conscious."

A fuzzy memory popped into my head. "Do I remember that you asked if Zardina talked to me about my taking charge of Rynstat?"

Leolie turned serious. "That was because Doric told me he wants you to be in charge of Rynstat."

I did not answer right away. "I think I know why."

"You do?"

"While I was on earth, Bennett had a few things he wanted me to tell you. His ghostly spirit hung around

Zardina for almost ten years without ever having been seen. That is how he knew she had hidden the enzyme formula here at Rynstat. The second issue involved Zardina and Doric."

"Bennett spied on Doric?"

"Let us just say Bennett was very loyal to Zardina, and rarely left her side."

"Okay," Leolie said. "So what did he want you to tell me?"

"Doric considered Zardina his most trusted commander. They met frequently. Both were getting on in age. In the last year or so they talked a lot about the future of Astrobia, specifically Astrobian leadership."

"Is that when they talked about you being in charge of Rynstat?"

"It is bigger than that," I said.

"How big?"

"You know how committed the Supreme Leader is to the science community. Well, Doric asked Zardina to identify the smartest and most trustworthy members of her team. She named you and me."

"Really?"

"Bennett said Doric wants you to be his second in command. That explains why he was so quick to name you as the new Science Commander following Zardina's death."

Leolie mouthed the word, 'me,' but no sound came out.

I placed a hand on her shoulder. "He wants you by his side so you can learn the job and replace him when he retires. He wants you to be the future Supreme Leader."

Leolie walked back to the console. "I have to sit down."

I followed her.

She looked up from her chair. "You are certain?"

I shrugged. "This is what Bennett told me. If it is true, then it would make sense that Doric wants me to be in charge of Rynstat, because he will transfer you to the Palace."

"I am not ready for a Palace assignment, let alone becoming the Supreme Leader."

"That is why he wants to train you."

"What if it is not true?" Leolie asked.

I stood a little taller and folded my arms across my chest. "Then I will refuse to command Rynstat."

"You cannot do that, Pidge. No one refuses the Supreme Leader."

I unfolded my arms. "I will do it diplomatically. I will talk about my affliction."

"What affliction? You mean you would lie?"

"It would not exactly be a lie. I am, after all, an alien on this planet."

"So, what do we do now?" Leolie asked.

"Well, we could just wait and keep asking, 'what do we do now?'. Or, you could contact Doric and let him know of my swift recovery. That my color is returning, and I look much better. Then he would feel free to tell you his plan."

"You really think so?"

"I have never seen you freeze up before, Leolie. You are actually showing fear. On Earth we would say, 'it's kinda cute.' " But if you are going to be my Supreme Leader, you will need to learn to get beyond your fears and act quickly."

"Okay, okay... Now get out of here so Doric will not see you when I video call him."

Fifty-Six

Leolie

I waited for Pidge to leave the observation chamber, then sent a video call to the Supreme Commander.

Doric's face appeared on the wall screen wearing a pilot's helmet and safety straps. His head was in constant motion, sweeping from side to side. He was obviously flying his transporter.

"Science Commander?" his voice boomed.

"I am calling as you requested, Supreme Leader, to report Pidge's remarkable improvement. She is doing well—walking around, taking nourishment, making complete sense."

"That is better than what Sittu told me."

"Pidge was asleep when he saw her."

"He neglected to mention that," Doric said. "That would explain why she was not walking, talking, or eating."

I did not know what to say. So I said nothing.

"Was there something else, Science Commander?"

*He did not say anything about a different assignment.
Quick, change the subject.* "Any findings of interest at
the mountain?"

"Nothing so far. Small volcano. Unpopulated area.
Air fire team on way to contain the forest fire."

"I will continue to monitor from Rynstat."

"Carry on. Doric, out."

That did not go very well. I glimpsed movement in
my peripheral vision.

Pidge walked in. "I heard everything. Guess he did
not have time to talk. I am certain he will contact you
after he returns from his mission."

I sighed. "Do not be so sure."

Pidge went to the wall screen and pointed to one of
the Lambou Mountain views. "This is the Wioa River,
the one Bennett flew over on his way back from the
volcano."

"And you know this because...?"

"Because he told me about a very unusual experience he had."

"Unusual?"

Pidge nodded. "Bennett said he flew into some sort
of trap about midway across this very river."

"Trap? I thought your Earth ghosts could penetrate
any object."

"Bennett said he thought the same thing. But he found himself in an invisible enclosure. One he could not escape from. He described the walls as supple but strong. He could see through them, but was bounced back every time he attempted to pass to the outside."

"There is no substance like that on Astrobia," I said.

"I agree. As far as he could tell, he had been trapped in a cylinder, closed on both ends, and large enough to hold a fully grown person."

"I know Bennett returned from Lambou Mountain because Sonny told me he had successfully planted the bomb," I said. "So, how did he escape?"

"This is where it gets even more interesting," Pidge said as she drew her finger across the river. "Bennett said he could feel the cylinder moving, and when he looked through the sides, he saw an adult male torvee on the river bank."

"A torvee?"

"Yes, and this one was standing on its hind legs and operating a hand-held device. A device that controlled the trap, and was bringing it in to him."

"Like an attraction-beam?" I asked.

Pidge nodded. "Bennett said he stopped right in front of the alien-torvee who must have opened the top of the cylinder. Bennett took the opportunity to slip out when he saw a torvee hand come toward him. Of course, the alien-torvee never saw Bennett's spirit. When Bennett looked back, he saw the alien-torvee's upper body disappear. Bennett thought the alien was climbing inside the cylinder looking for a trapped bird to eat."

"Fascinating. So we have another alien disguised as a torvee."

"Or maybe the same one I saw entering the science building?"

"But Pidge, we never saw that torvee leave."

Pidge walked back to the console and stood across from me. "I have been thinking about that. What if the alien had the container with him? He could load it up with prize elements and float it through the halls."

I sat back. "Okay. But even at night, someone would have seen him, as well as the prize elements that would seem to be hanging in the air."

"Thought about that too. What if Bennett was wrong about the container being invisible? What if it was reflective instead?"

"Reflective?"

Pidge put both hands on the console and leaned forward. "Think about it, Leolie. If the material of the outside of the cylinder were reflective, Bennett would only have seen a mirrored image of sky, trees, and water. He would have believed nothing was there. That would also explain why the torvee had to stick his hand inside the container to search for a captured bird, because he could not see through the material from the outside."

"Okay," I said. "That might explain why no one saw the prized elements floating down the hallway of the Science Building, but they could still see the torvee. And the torvee would still have had to open the door to float the container outside. And remember, you never saw him come out."

Pidge shook her head. "That is as far as I got in my thinking."

I saw movement on the wall screen and pointed. "The torvee!"

We watched as the orange colored adult male torvee moved on four legs in typical ape-like fashion from the tree line. At the river's edge he stopped, looked around, and stood on his hind legs.

"Ellie," I said.

"Yes, Leolie."

"Power five."

"Confirm power five."

The camera zoomed in, and we could see that the alien held a small gray box as he looked toward the river.

Pidge hurried to the wall screen. "I think he is doing it. He is retrieving the container, just as Bennett described."

"Watch carefully, Pidge. If you are correct about the reflectivity, we should catch the reflection of the torvee when he brings the container to the riverbank, like he is looking at a mirror."

Pidge pointed. "There! Looks like two torvees, facing each other."

"Yes. Unmistakably his reflection. Well done, Pidge. Brilliant."

"I cannot see his arm. He must be sticking it inside the container," Pidge said. ... "Look! He has a blue xeffen by the neck. Birds are definitely not part of a real torvee's diet."

"Pidge, you and I need to get out there. Contact a trainer from the Science Academy and have them send their top student to monitor this console while we are gone."

"Will do," Pidge said as she moved to the door.

I tapped the transmitter on my belt. "Leolie calling General Xigryn. Do you copy?"

"Xigryn here."

"I need your help, General."

"I am at your service, Science Commander."

"I believe we have spotted an alien, southeast of Lambou Mountain."

"An alien? But how...?"

"You will need your best detection equipment, a detainment room, and a few of your troops."

"Who, or what are we looking for?"

"You are looking for a shape-shifter, General. This one appears as an adult male torvee. He has an invisible container large enough to conceal himself and a stash of our prized elements."

"My kind of challenge."

"Can you pick up Pidge and me at Rynstat on the way?"

"Copy. Xigryn, out."

Whoosh...Whoosh.

Pidge stuck her head in the chamber. "That will be the eleven-year old from the Academy. I will bring her in."

I heard a distinct thump-clop, thump-clop, thump-clop. A young girl appeared in the doorway leaning on crutches, her right leg in a yellow cast. As with all Astrobian children, her coloring had not yet been fully established—light green skin, maroon hair, brown eyes surrounded by aqua.

She dropped her head in a bow, then looked up confidently. "I am Foreen. I was instructed to report to Science Commander Leolie."

"I am Leolie," I said as I stood and motioned for her to sit in my chair.

Foreen shook her head. "I could not use your chair, Science Commander."

Pidge looked at me and smiled.

I walked to the youngster.

Foreen's bright eyes never left mine.

"We will be leaving Rynstat. You are to monitor the screens while we are gone. The chair belongs to whoever is using the console. That means, until we return, the chair belongs to you. Do you understand?"

"Yes, Science Commander."

I put my hand on her back and walked with her as she 'thump-clopped' to the console.

Foreen plopped into the chair and laid her crutches on the floor. She scanned the console.

"Ellie, Foreen will be monitoring the console. She will have questions."

"Understood," Ellie said. "Hello, Foreen."

"Hello, Ellie."

I pointed at the wall screen. "See the middle view? The one with the river?"

Foreen nodded.

"It is on power-five so we can see every detail. That is where we will be, searching for a torvee. You are to watch that view constantly."

"Yes, Science Commander."

"I may contact you from there."

Foreen pointed at the small screen on the console. "A large transport is landing outside."

"That will be our ride."

Fifty-Seven

Breanne

Grams looked at the wall clock and stood up. "It's after five. Time to get y'all home."

Sonny and I scooted our chairs back.

Mrs. Pidgeon stood. "Can't you stay? Just a little longer?"

"We need to go, Marge," Grams said as she led us around the table to say our goodbyes.

Mrs. Pidgeon got all emotional—crying, holding Pidge's transmitter to her heart. "Times like these, saying thank you is just not enough. You all have changed my life." She looked at me. "Not just changed my life, but you saved my life." She wrapped me up in a warm hug.

I looked down at her. "You saved me, too. I'd be in Astrobia if you and Grams hadn't held me down."

Mrs. Pidgeon released me and grabbed Sonny, pinning his arms to his side. "Thank you for bringing my Pidge back to me. She never would have survived the portal without you."

Sonny looked away.

Mrs. Pidgeon pulled Grams into her. "We have a bond that will never be broken."

I couldn't hear what Grams said, but tears rolled down her cheeks.

We left the library in silence. When we pushed through the school door we saw that the driver-side door of Grams' car was open. She had been in such a rush to find out about Sonny that she never closed it.

Sonny tossed his backpack in the front and climbed in. I threw mine on the backseat and slid in beside it.

We were all exhausted. No one said a word. Grams dropped me off at my house. I raised a hand goodbye and Sonny did likewise. I half-carried and half-dragged my backpack with one hand, and bounced it up the porch steps.

Momma opened the front door and took my backpack. "My word. Your clothes, your hair, your glasses. You look like you've been in a fight. What happened?

I don't want Mrs. Pidgeon to get in trouble. I promised. I can't tell Momma that Grams tackled me and that she and Mrs. Pidgeon wrestled me to keep from going to the portal. "I think Mrs. Pidgeon had a heart attack," I said. "She was lying on the floor with her hand on her chest. She could barely talk. I had to help her."

"What?" Momma guided me to a kitchen chair. "What happened? Is she okay?"

"She's okay now. I got her purse and she took a pill. She got better pretty fast."

"Thank goodness." She took my face in her hands. "It's a blessing you were there. You saved her life."

I forced a tight smile.

"I'm so proud of you. ... Now I see why you look so tired. You must've been scared silly. I can't even imagine." She glanced at the oven. "We won't be eating for a while. How about I take you up to your room so you can lie down? You can tell me all about it after you've had a nap."

I rubbed my throbbing shoulder. "That would be nice."

Momma put her arm around me and walked me up the stairs and into my bedroom. I put my broken glasses on the end table and sat on the bed. Momma took my shoes off, picked up my legs and swung them onto the bed. Her kissing me on the forehead was the last thing I remember before falling asleep.

The dream began in the school library. No matter the size, every book on the shelves—big ones, small ones, thin or thick ones—was red. I drifted in the air through the aisles as if I were a spirit, searching for just the right book. But I wasn't using my eyes. I was seeing with my mind. I sensed something far in the distance. It drew me like a magnet.

I floated down two more aisles before I could be certain. ... Yes. I sensed it like a long lost memory. Not a word or a place, but a feeling. A strong feeling. An overwhelming feeling—fear.

I began breathing faster, almost panting. Both the attraction and the fear grew stronger, pulling me more quickly until I stopped in front a small red book. I could 'see' it glowing in my mind's eye. It lifted from the shelf, then opened right in front of me.

"Help!"

The voice was familiar. But whose?

"Bree! Where are you?"

Only my family calls me Bree. No. Wait. Sonny calls me Bree. "Sonny? That you?"

"Bree! Help me!"

The red book snapped shut, zipped across the room to the transom window, and stopped.

I glided over and reached for it. As soon as I touched it, the red book pulled me through the window. I found myself racing at hurricane speed through the portal.

A light appeared in the distance. Two people suddenly popped out of that light. We zoomed toward each other like two Air Force fighter jets.

In a blur I saw Sonny, his arms wrapped around Pidge. The red book jumped from my hands and chased after them. I kept going.

"Nooo! Sonny! Help!"

My entire body shook. I couldn't stop it.

"Bree, honey. It's okay. Everything's okay. It's just a dream."

I opened my eyes to find Momma gently shaking me. Daddy stood behind her.

"You're soaking wet," Momma said, "and trembling like a leaf."

She put her arms around me.

I felt my heart pounding against my ribs. I needed to catch my breath.

Momma turned to Daddy. "Mrs. Pidgeon almost dying must have really scared her. Bring me a cold wet washcloth."

Daddy came back in the room and handed the washcloth to Momma. She gently wiped my face and then the back of my neck.

It felt soooo good.

Fifty-Eight

Sonny

My whole body ached from hanging onto Pidge in the portal and then crashing to the floor, even with a mattress.

It was so hard to walk, like my shoes were made of lead. Even harder to climb the porch steps. My head seemed to be filled with cotton, blocking any thoughts. If I had an idea it soon disappeared, never to be heard from again. I waited at the front door for Grams.

She came up behind me with the key. She looked super tired, hunched forward. Her hand shook as she struggled to stick the door key in the lock.

I tried to picture her tackling Bree. That musta been something. I've never seen Grams even sit on the floor, let alone wrestle someone way bigger than her.

Grams shooed me up to my bedroom to lie down.

I plodded up the stairs and did a Superman flop on my bed, face down, shoes and all. I flipped my glasses off and immediately fell asleep.

In the dream I felt myself flying. My arms hurt while I carried something? No. Not something. It was Pidge. My bodied tensed as I pulled with all my might to keep her close, to keep her safe. I needed to take a breath, but the pressure of the portal was so strong I couldn't breathe.

Then I saw Bree coming at us from the Memphis portal.

Huh? What's she doin' in here?

"No! Go back, Bree! Go back!"

I woke up. My arms wrapped around my pillow. I looked to make sure my pillow wasn't Pidge. I patted around for my glasses but couldn't find them.

I felt a hand on my back. "It's okay, Sonny."

I rolled over to find Grams.

She held out my glasses. "Bad dream?"

"Yeah." I let loose of the pillow, sat up, and slid my glasses on. "I was in the portal holding Pidge. But Breanne was in there too. Goin' to Astrobia."

"Truth is that almost happened."

"And she would have gone there if you hadn't tackled her, right?"

Grams nodded. "And if Marge hadn't been holdin' her legs I think she woulda got clean away from me.

But she didn't. And now she's safe in her home. So how 'bout we go downstairs and get some supper?"

I slid off the bed.

Grams put an arm around me and we went down the stairs side-by-side.

Fifty-Nine

Leolie

General Xigryn arrived in a large military transporter. Once inside, he gave Pidge and me a brief introduction to his ship. The cockpit was about ten times as big as my personal transporter. It had a large instrument panel and two side-by-side seats up front, with a fold-down seat behind each one.

Xigryn gestured to rows of seats in the mid-cabin. "We can carry a full company of troops. Today, I only brought one squad—six of our best soldiers."

The soldiers sat rigid, facing forward, as if at attention.

Xigryn pointed over them, to the rear of the plane. "This transport has a huge cargo hold. We have adapted the lower bay to contain large animals. That should be big enough for our shape shifter."

I handed the general a slip of paper. "Here are the coordinates of our destination. We need to get there quickly. I can explain what I think is happening on the way."

The general led us to the cockpit. He took the co-pilot seat and punched in the coordinates. Pidge and I sat in the fold-down seats, and buckled our safety straps. Within seconds we had lifted off and were at full speed.

Xigryn looked back at me. "The more I know, the better able my troops and I will be able to capture this alien."

I nodded. "The Supreme Leader is heading up an investigation at Lambou Mountain. We pulled up surrounding views of the area on our wall screen to assist. Most views focused on the mountain itself and on the main lava flow into the forest. One contained a section of the Wioa River, just southeast of the mountain. Pidge saw movement. I increased the power to get a better look. Turned out to be an adult male torvee."

"That's odd," Xigryn said. "I have never seen torvees that far north."

Pidge jumped in. "Yes, General. And how many of them have you seen that walk around on their hind legs?"

"Only for short distances."

"That's what we thought," I said. "So, I zoomed in for a closer look. Not only did this torvee walk on his hind legs, but he held a small gray-colored box in one hand."

"You think this torvee is an alien? A shape shifter?"

"That is what we need to determine," I said. "But, there is one more thing to consider."

"Yes," Pidge said, thrusting her arm toward the General. "The torvee held the gray box out in front of him, above the river. All of sudden, there were two male torvees on screen."

"You mean a second torvee just appeared out of nowhere?" Xigryn asked.

Pidge nodded. "The second torvee popped up right in front of the other one."

"But Pidge figured it out," I said. "The second torvee was only a reflection of the first torvee."

"A reflection? A reflection off what?"

"The torvee's reflection could only have come from an object large enough to show the entire torvee," Pidge said.

"But," I added. "We could not see any such object."

"My hypothesis," Pidge said, "was that the object must be covered in reflective material. And that reflectivity made it essentially invisible."

"And sure enough," I said. "The torvee's arm disappeared for a few seconds before it reappeared holding a blue xeffen by the neck."

"So the bird had been inside the invisible container," Xigryn said. "That container is what you want me to find."

"Exactly," I said.

The transporter slowed.

"General," the pilot said. "The designated area is right below us."

Xigryn turned to the front.

We strained to see out the forward windshield.

Xigryn pointed. "There he is. Looks like the torvee has almost finished eating the xeffen."

Pidge and I unbuckled our safety straps and moved up to get a better look.

"I cannot see the container," Pidge said. "But the gray box is on the ground beside the torvee."

The torvee looked up and dropped the feathered xeffen carcass. He grabbed the gray box and twisted around, pointing it in the air. Then, we watched the torvee disappear—first the feet, then the body, and finally the head."

"He is inside the container," I said.

Xigryn began clicking buttons. An image appeared on his screen—a large cylinder. "Got him," he said. "Bay doors open," Xigryn ordered.

"Yes, General," the pilot said.

"The cylinder is moving away. Quickly. Attraction beam on."

"Attraction beam on, General."

The image of the cylinder stopped, then floated up to the transporter.

"Bay doors closed," Xigryn ordered.

"Bay doors closed, General."

The transporter settled on the ground. Xigryn released his safety straps, and moved quickly to the mid-cabin. We followed.

He spoke to his soldiers. "An alien and his container-transporter have been acquired and are now in the lower bay. He appears as a torvee, but we believe he is a shape shifter and could take many forms. The outside of the container is made of reflective material making it seem invisible."

The squad stood in unison.

Xigryn pointed. "You two. You are responsible for spraying the outside of the container."

"Yes, General," they said as one.

"The rest of you set your weapons to stun."

"Yes, General," they said.

"We do not know how dangerous this alien is, but I want him alive."

The squad trailed behind Xigryn to the back of the transporter and down a staircase to the lower bay.

Pidge and I followed. The bay looked empty.

Xigryn pointed with both hands and two solders moved forward, one on each side of the bay. They opened their canisters and began spraying. Within seconds a green cylinder appeared, about eight feet in length and three feet in diameter. Then a handle became visible on the end nearest us.

A third soldier grabbed the handle, and looked back at the General. The three remaining soldiers knelt on one knee with their weapons aimed at the door.

Xigryn gave a quick hand signal. The soldier pulled the handle and stepped back, swinging the door completely open. The inside was dark.

"Light it up!" Xigryn ordered.

Bright lights streamed from the underside of each soldier's weapon and filled the cylinder.

No torvee.

Instead we saw a blue bird perched on top of a mound of rocks—a xeffen.

Xigryn pointed to the soldier in the middle and waved him forward. The soldier crouched and entered the cylinder. We heard the soft buzz of his weapon. In less than a minute he walked out of the cylinder, an unconscious blue xeffen cradled in his arms.

Xigryn pointed. "Take the bird to the first containment box." "You three go inside and carefully check everything," he ordered. "Look for the smallest insect. This shape shifter could have taken any form." He turned to the remaining soldiers. "You two, make sure no living thing comes out of that cylinder without your firing on it."

Pidge stood behind the two soldiers and strained to see what was happening inside.

I followed the first soldier as he carried the bird into the containment box—an enormous cube made of thick unbreakable glass walls and ceiling—able to hold our largest animals. He placed the bird on the floor in the middle of the cube, then backed out and secured the massive door.

Get it!

Buzz!

I turned to see two of the soldiers bent over, studying something on the floor. One looked up.

"Got a spider here," he reported, holding it up. The unconscious spider more than filled the soldier's two hands. Its brilliant red and green iridescent colors warned all predators to stay away.

"Take the spider to the other containment box," Xigryn said. "The rest of you, keep looking."

The soldiers removed everything from the cylinder. A pile of jagged rocks and silver-colored dust sat in front of the cylinder.

"No more birds, animals or insects, General," one soldier said, handing him the gray control box. "Only this box and those rocks."

I walked over and grabbed a few rocks, then looked back at Xigryn. "These are prized elements, General. Stolen prized elements."

Pidge yelled, "Got movement over here." I turned to see Pidge's face almost touching the glass as she watched the spider.

Xigryn and I joined her. A few of the spider's twelve legs were twitching. It tried to stand, but half the legs still were asleep. The spider collapsed on its belly. I glanced over at the other box. The xeffen remained unconscious.

When I looked back, the spider had succeeded in standing, but it was a little wobbly.

"Have any experience with shape-shifters?" Xigryn asked.

Pidge and I both shook our heads.

"Well, I have. All I can say is that anything is possible. Some shape-shifters always stay in the form of a person, just change appearance and size. Sometimes they can change from men to women. Some can change into animals, birds or insects. That makes it easy for them to get in and out of small places."

"Of course," Pidge said, "if you just changed into a spider someone might come along and step on you."

"Indeed," Xigryn said. "Still there are other shifters who seem to melt before your eyes, changing into a liquid. Good for escaping."

"What do you think we have here?" I asked, nodding at the spider.

Xigryn rubbed his chin. "Well, we know it was a male torvee." He glanced at the xeffen and back at the spider. "And we are pretty sure it can change to either a spider or a bird. So maybe its shifting is limited to the non-person realm."

"Seems to me," Pidge said, "this shifter has to be able to operate that cylinder. So it needs fingers to work the controls on the gray box."

"And," I said, "it has to be big enough to open the large bins in the Science Building and dig out the prized elements. Size and hands make a torvee the perfect animal to shape shift into."

Pidge pointed. "The spider is walking around. Seems to be exploring its new surroundings."

"My experience tells me this spider is dangerous. But it is merely a spider," Xigryn said. "We need to be watching the bird."

We moved to the first containment box where the blue xeffen lie on its side. The bird began to move as soon as we arrived. First one leg, then the other. Its head lifted off the floor and turned slowly from side to side. Its whole body quivered. Finally, after several attempts, it stood. More certain of its balance, the bird opened its wings and flapped them vigorously, but did not leave the floor.

"Looks like he is checking to see if all his parts are working," Xigryn said.

All six of the soldiers were now standing behind us watching the bird.

The bird's head jerked around. It stared up at us for three or four seconds before it began backing up to the far side of the box. Suddenly, it bent its legs, stretched its wings and sprang into the air.

Thump!

It crashed into the glass ceiling and fell to the floor.
The bird scrambled to its feet and took off again, this
time for the side.

Thump!

Another crash. It slid down the side wall to the floor.
The bird appeared to be stunned. It took its time standing. It looked at the line of Astrobians, then dropped
its head.

"I think he is giving up," Pidge said. "He cannot get
away and he is greatly outnumbered."

We watched as the bird began to get larger. Legs
lengthened and thickened. Bird claws turned into feet.
Wings morphed into arms and hands. The bird's sharp
beak softened and shrank into a person's nose. And
the feathers somehow became clothes. We were wit-
nessing the development of a new life form.

Before us was an interesting figure. A tall, thin male
with pale yellow skin. Probably a foot taller than me.
A small, rather flat nose. A thumb and four extra long
fingers on each hand. Bald with what appeared to be
two short antennae sticking up from the top of his
head.

"A male, from the planet Gari," Xigryn said, sound-
ing a hard 'g' and rolling the 'r.' "By the lack of yellow
in his skin, I would say he is rather elderly."

"Elderly, like he came here as an old Garian? Or like he has been on Astrobia for a while without the W-35 enzyme?"

"I cannot say. But I am certain he can tell us."

Sixty

Leolie

Xigryn's radio chirped. "General," the pilot said. "The Supreme Leader's transporter is setting down beside us."

"Open the rear bay door and lower the ramp," Xigryn said. He looked at Pidge and me. "Ready?"

I nodded. "Lead the way, General."

We turned from the containment box and walked to the tail of the big transporter. The large door had opened upward and the end of the ramp was just settling onto the ground. A small figure approached dressed in a bright red and green uniform. Two taller females followed wearing camouflage military fatigues. We waited at the top of the ramp. We bowed our heads as the Supreme Leader came near.

Doric offered no greeting. "Why are you here?"

I stepped forward. "While monitoring the area we saw a torvee acting very strangely. We thought it might be a shape-shifter. I contacted General Xigryn for assistance."

"And?" Doric said impatiently.

"The General and his men picked him up," I said, motioning behind me.

Doric strode through us. "Show me what you captured."

The three of us wheeled and hurried to keep up with Doric. His guards fell in behind us. He stopped at the containment cube holding the spider. "That him?"

"No Supreme Leader," I said. "We found two life forms. Thought it best to contain each one until we were sure. The shape-shifter is in the next containment cube."

Doric turned and strode to the first cube. "Ah, Gari," he said, turning to Xigryn. "We have not seen one of these for years, right, General?"

Xigryn bowed his head. "It has been a long time, Supreme Leader."

"How did you find him?" Doric asked.

Xigryn pointed to Pidge and me. "They found him, and his invisible container."

"Doric looked behind him. "That thing there? Does not look invisible to me."

"That is because we sprayed the cylinder, so we could see what we were dealing with," Xigryn said.

Doric nodded.

I spoke up. "Pidge and I were monitoring the volcano area when we saw a torvee eating a blue xeffen and holding a small control box."

"Not things one would expect a torvee to be doing," Doric said.

"That is why I called General Xigryn. He was able to capture the shape-shifter and the invisible cylinder he traveled in. Turned out the cylinder also contained some of our prized elements."

"Prized elements!" Doric snapped. "You mean from the Science Building? Did he cause the explosion?"

"We do not know, Supreme Leader," I said.

Just then the shape-shifter approached us and began speaking in his home language.

"How is your Gari, General?" Doric asked. "Think you can translate, or do we need to use a decipher device?"

"I am afraid it has been too long," Xigryn said. "I will switch on the decipher device."

The voice on the device was that of a female which made me wonder if the person inside the cube was really a male. Her words came in spurts as the Gari spoke, then waited for the translation.

"My name is Bin ... I am Jarai from the planet Gari ... I have been here for two and a half of your years ... Our planet is in desperate need of prized elements ...

Yes, I stole them ... I have been trying to get home ... but have been unable to pass through the portal."

"How many Gari are on this planet?" Doric asked.

"I know of only two ... me and Yalik."

"Did either you or Yalik blow up our Science Building?"

Bin shook his head. "We would not do that ... We need your prized elements."

"Where is Yalik?"

"I have not seen or heard from him since the explosion."

"Take him to the palace dungeon," Doric ordered. "I will talk with him later."

"Yes, Supreme leader," Xigryn said with a bow of his head.

Doric turned to Pidge and me. "I will take you back to Rynstat."

We bowed and followed him to his transporter. Once inside, the two guards took the fold-down seats in the cockpit. Doric touched his co-pilot's shoulder. "Set the coordinates for Rynstat. I will be in the passenger cabin."

The co-pilot nodded. "Yes, Supreme Leader. Rynstat."

Doric closed the cockpit door and motioned for us to sit with him in the small passenger area. He looked Pidge over from head to toe. "You certainly appear to be healthy."

"Things were difficult for a while," Pidge said. "But I have recovered. I feel strong now."

"Good," Doric said. "Because I want you to be the new Science Commander."

Pidge looked at me then back at Doric. "With all respect, Supreme Leader, that is Leolie's job."

"Your loyalty is commendable, Pidge," Doric said. "But I have a new assignment for Leolie. One that will still allow you to report to her."

Then Doric turned to me. "I am impressed with the way you two identified the shape-shifter. And I must say, Zardina had the utmost regard for your loyalty and your skills."

"Thank you, Supreme Leader," I said.

"I need someone I can trust," Doric said. "Someone whose council I can depend on. Leolie, I want you with me in the palace."

I bowed my head. "It will be an honor."

"So it is done," Doric said. "I will expect you to move to the palace by the rise of second moon."

"I will be there," I said. I snuck a glance at Pidge. She was smiling. And me? ... I was *HAPPY*.

Sixty-One

Sonny

I couldn't believe it when I opened my eyes Sunday morning, it was almost ten o'clock. I don't remember sleeping that long before. I heard the wooden squeak of a chair and turned to see Grams sitting by the door. I found my glasses and sat up.

"Anything wrong?" I asked.

Grams wore her nightgown. She looked tired and spoke slowly. "Nothin' wrong, child. Just checkin' on you."

"How long you been here?"

"For a spell. Makin' sure you was okay." She grinned. "Makin' sure you was still here."

Huh? Oh, yeah. I glanced around the room. *Still on Earth.* I stretched. "I was really out. I don't think I even dreamed."

Grams nodded slowly. "Yesterday was a big day. For all of us."

"Grams? Are you okay?"

She smiled. "My arther-itis is talkin' to me, but I'll be fine."

"I didn't know you could read minds."

"Don't think I can do that. But have to admit my Grammy musta passed somethin' down to me, cause when I held hands with Breanne, I was aware of your feelings. Darndest thing. Never woulda thought I could do it from across the room, let alone all the way through outer space."

I chill ran through my body. "I'm so glad you did. I was so scared. I didn't think I'd ever see anyone again. I wouldn't have made it without reading your thoughts."

Grams' eyes filled with tears. "And I wouldn't have made it without you coming back to me." She took her glasses off and wiped her eyes on her sleeve. "Let's get dressed. I'll make us some breakfast."

Breakfast tasted better than ever. We did the dishes—I washed, Grams dried. Afterward, I went up to my room.

I felt funny—something about the way I was thinking. I'd only been on Astrobia for a few hours and eaten one strange vegetable, but I couldn't shake the feeling that I was different—that I had changed.

I turned on my computer. 'The Code Breaker' site was flashing.

I wonder... I clicked on the icon and watched a detailed drawing of a fortress fill the screen. The voice of an unseen announcer boomed as questions flashed on the screen:

» Can you get inside?
» Can you break the coded message and discover the keypad's passcode?
» Can you do it before the keypad explodes?
» Can you do it twice—once to get in the door and a second time to access the nine-carat diamond?
» You will have only sixty-seconds to enter the correct passcode.
» Ready?

Let's see what happens. I moved my avatar to the massive wooden door and had him flip open the keypad.

The coded message flashed on the screen: **61905294**

I winced as a piercing siren began to wail and a digital clock counted down. I forced myself to lean forward into the noise, as if I were trying to balance myself in a wind tunnel.

57 seconds left.

Concentrate. ... No obvious pattern. ... I need four single-digit numbers for the keypad.

50 seconds.

Eight numbers in the coded message. There're four pairs: 61, 90, 52, 94

43 seconds.

Nothing there. Reverse each pair: 16, 09, 25, 49

40 seconds.

Yeah! Perfect squares. The square root of each pair: 4, 3, 5, 7

32 seconds.

I punched in 4 3 5 7.

29 seconds.

The siren continued. The door didn't open. *Think! ... Reverse the numbers:* 7 5 3 4

22 seconds.

I punched in 7 5 3 4.

Silence. The clock froze on "18."

Got it!

I heard a loud metallic click. The door swung open.

I'd never been here before. *Cool.*

I took two deep breaths then moved my avatar through the door and into the foyer. A red keypad sat atop a waist-high stand directly in front of him. Behind it, the huge nine-carat diamond sparkled, encased in a large glass box.

I had my avatar grab an aerosol can and spray the room. Just beyond the keypad, red laser lines appeared crisscrossing the large foyer from every angle. *No way through all that.* I focused on the keypad.

The instant my avatar flipped open the keypad cover, my senses were bombarded with that same piercing siren. The countdown clock already at 59 seconds.

Inside the keypad cover was the coded message:

R S V P

52 seconds.

Letters? I glanced at the keypad. *I need numbers. Quick, count each letter's placement in the alphabet: 18 for R, 19 for S, 22 for V, and 16 for P.*

That translates to 18, 19, 22, 16

43 seconds.

No pattern. No consistent divisor. Only one squared number.

38 seconds.

Reverse each pair: 81, 91, 12, 61. *Nothing.*

33 seconds.

Go back. R, S, V, P … Check the phone pad for num-bers matching each letter. I pulled out my cell: R=7, S=7, V=8, P=7.

23 seconds.

That has to be it. I punched in 7 7 8 7

Silence!

My body jerked forward when the siren suddenly stopped.

A rumbling sound as the stand lowered into the floor and the glass case lifted up, away from the diamond. I urged my avatar forward. The diamond jumped to his hand. Church bells chimed. Confetti covered the screen and came together to form words:

CONGRATULAIONS SONNY ELLIOTT!
YOU HAVE RECAPTURED THE STOLEN DIAMOND.

I just sat there, staring at the screen. Only a few days ago I had not been able to solve the first coded message. Now, I broke both codes with time to spare. *Maybe something did happen to me on Astrobia.*

Sixty-Two

Sonny

Monday morning, after breakfast, I swung into my backpack to leave for school.

Grams came over and hugged me. "Don't you dare go anywhere near that transom window. Promise me."

"I promise."

"You come straight home after school, hear?"

"I will."

I looked back after I'd walked about half 'a block. Grams was still on the porch watching me. I gave her a quick wave.

She waved back.

Breanne was waiting at the corner when I got there. Her green glasses had been patched up with tape. "Hey, Sonny. You okay?"

I nodded. "Yeah." I could tell she was just bursting to say something. "You?"

"I am now...now you're here."

Then she told me all about her dream of passing me in the portal.

"No kiddin'," I said. "I had the same dream, but without the red book."

Breanne looked down and spoke softly. "I was afraid I'd never see you again."

"Same for me."

She looked at me. "Really?"

I nodded.

"I've never had the same dream as someone else," she said. "What does it mean?"

"Don't know. Must have something to do with our reading each other's mind between Earth and Astrobia. Maybe we were trying so hard that now we share some of the same brain patterns or something."

"That's freaky."

We started walking to school, but without talking. Odd. We weren't reading each other's mind either. Guess we were kinda in a daze. The next thing I knew, Bree was holding the door for me. I walked in and was surprised to hear all the usual noise of kids talking and locker doors banging. It sounded great.

"We have to check on Mrs. Pidgeon," Breanne said. "I hope her heart is okay."

As usual, teachers stood outside their classrooms to welcome their students and to keep an eye on the kids in the hall. We found Mrs. Pidgeon standing beside the library door.

Her face lit up when she saw us. "Oh, there you are. I was hoping to see you this morning."

"How're you feeling?" Breanne asked. "I mean your heart."

Mrs. Pidgeon smiled. "How sweet of you to ask. I am doing just fine. And how about the two of you?

Breanne looked over at me. "We're okay. Just had some scary dreams."

"Perfectly understandable," Mrs. Pidgeon said. "I had a few myself. We certainly had an intensely emotional day."

I spoke up. "My Grams told me to give you her best."

"Thank you, Sonny," Mrs. Pidgeon said. "I couldn't have made it without her. Please tell her I will call her later."

I nodded.

Mrs. Pidgeon looked around, leaned forward to me and spoke softly. "Could you help with the, er, radio? I don't want to mess anything up next Saturday."

"Sure."

We followed her inside. She pulled Pidge's two-way radio from her desk drawer. I showed her the call and receive buttons.

Mrs. Pidgeon held out the two-way. "Pidge said she would send a single ping."

"Right," I said. "And you are to ping her back by touching it right here—one ping if people are around, two pings if you are alone. When you are alone she will talk to you."

A few students came in.

"Thank you, Sonny," Mrs. Pidgeon said. "I will let you know how it works out."

Sixty-Three

Breanne

The next day after school, Sonny and I walked out of the building and found Grandpa waiting in his car. We climbed into the backseat.

"Things have moved quickly on our cold case," Grandpa said, turning around to talk to us. "I thought you two would like to be involved. And before you ask— yes, I have talked to your mother, Breanne, and your grandmother, Sonny. They are okay with you coming with me."

"What's goin' on, Mr. Thurman?" Sonny asked.

"The lab was able to match the paint on Mr. Sanh's clothes to a color used on the Mercedes-Benz E Class."

"Wow, really?" Sonny said. "But there must be lots of those around town."

"There are indeed. But, it turns out this is a light blue paint called 'Quartz Blue.' Mercedes only used that paint color on their 2010, 2011, and 2012 models. That narrowed down our search."

"What kind of search?" I asked.

"One done on a computer," Grandpa said. "Police pulled up a list of all the 2010 to 2012 Quartz Blue E Class Mercedes-Benzes that were registered in Shelby County back in 2015."

"Because 2015 is when Mr. Sanh and Con went missing," I said.

"That's right, partner," Grandpa said. "Now tell me what's the next step?"

"You have a list of owners," Sonny said. "Now you can go interview each one."

"Okay...," Grandpa said, "but that's still a large number of people. Where should we start?"

"Just go in alphabetical order," Sonny said.

For a second, I musta thought I was in class. I raised my hand and bumped into the car's ceiling. They laughed. Me too.

"Okay, Breanne," Grandpa said, still smiling. "I take it you don't think we should begin with the letter A."

This time, I didn't raise my hand. "We should start with the people the officers interviewed in the beginning."

"You're on the right track," Grandpa said. "Sonny?"

"Using the computer, I bet you could find the person who was interviewed back in 2015 and owned a blue Mercedes."

"Excellent! Yes, and that's precisely what the police did."

"Did they get a match?" I asked.

Grandpa held up a finger. "One match. A man who, like Mr. Sanh, worked for Winchester Bank and Trust. A man who was also a regional bank manager, and was in competition with Mr. Sanh for a promotion to Central Bank Manager."

"Was he the one that did it?" Sonny asked.

"He's definitely the one," Grandpa said.

"Are we going to arrest him?" I asked.

Grandpa shook his head. "He's already been arrested. Turns out he's been feeling guilty all this time. He confessed the minute the detective showed up at his house. Said he'd been planning for a month how to run Mr. Sanh over with his car. Even dug the grave ahead of time. Then he waited for days until Mr. Sanh walked down the street by that wooded area."

"We got him," I said.

"We sure did," Grandpa said. "And there's more. He told the detective he was glad to be arrested because his house was haunted by the ghost of Nguyen Kim Sanh."

Sonny looked at me. "You think Mr. Sanh's ghost attached itself to the man's car, or maybe his shovel. Then was taken home by him?"

"Either that," Grandpa said, "or the man has a major guilty conscience that's made him see and hear things that aren't there."

"Sick," I said.

Grandpa made a face. "Sick?"

"That means very cool," Sonny said.

"If that man's been arrested, where are you taking us?" I asked.

"Thought you'd like to come with me to his house so you could talk to Mr. Sanh yourselves," Grandpa said.

"That'd be straight fire," Sonny said.

"Don't tell me," Grandpa said. "That means 'cool,' too."

"Very, very cool," Sonny said.

"But can we pick up Con first?" I asked.

Grandpa swiveled around and started the car. "I thought you'd never ask."

Grandpa drove to the Central Gardens neighborhood. Sure enough, Con was stretched out above her favorite fire hydrant. Sonny rolled down the window and called her. Con popped to her feet and zoomed right through the door into the car.

"She's in, Grandpa," I said, almost yelling. "Standing above the backseat, right between Sonny and me. She's barking so loud, you must be able to hear her."

Grandpa put the car in gear. "Afraid not. Don't hear a thing."

We drove east for about twenty-five minutes until we arrived in a Cordova neighborhood on the northeast side of Memphis—wide streets, nice yards, but no sidewalks. Grandpa pulled up a steep driveway of a one-story red brick house and got out of the car.

Con fidgeted, whimpered, then dropped to a lying position just above the backseat.

"What's up with Con," Sonny asked. "She's acting like she's scared."

"This is a whole new place for her," I said, "maybe she needs to be attached to one of us."

I let go of Sonny's hand and held my arms out in front like when I carry my folded clothes upstairs. "Come-on, Con. I'll carry you. I couldn't see her, but following the sound of her whimpering I knew she had floated into my arms.

Grandpa led us to the porch where he pulled a key from his pocket and unlocked the front door. He stepped inside and switched on a light. Before we could join him, Con began barking loudly. I could tell by the sound that she'd left me and was zooming through the house. After we got inside I took Sonny's hand.

Sonny looked at me. "Hear that? Con's changed her bark. She's yipping like she's playing with something."

I nodded. "Or with someone."

"Think she found Mr. Sanh?"

"Guess we'll know pretty soon."

We waited for several minutes. Then Con started barking—strong and getting louder. We looked in the direction of her bark. Con's head, then her body, flashed through the wall. She sailed into my arms.

"Wait, Con," a man's voice said. "We've just seen each other for the first time in four years, and now you're running away from me?"

The ghost of a man appeared through the same wall, then stopped when he saw us.

"Hello, Mr. Sanh," I said.

Con leapt from my arms and returned to Mr. Sanh.

"You can see me?" Sanh asked.

"Sure can," Sonny said.

"Well, I'll be," Sanh said. "And you're holding hands. How very strange."

"I'm Breanne. This is Sonny. When we touch we are able to see and hear spirits." I pointed. "And this is my Grandpa. He's a retired policeman. He's the one who solved your case. But he can't see or hear you."

"Good to meet you, Mr. Sanh," Grandpa said.

Mr. Sanh gave a small bow. "It is entirely my pleasure, kind sir. I am forever in your debt."

I told Grandpa what Mr. Sanh said.

Grandpa shook his head. "I couldn't have done it without these two. They found Con. Then Con led us to your grave. The rest was just basic police work."

"No wonder Con was so set on getting me to follow her. She too, is in your debt."

It was hard to tell where Con's form ended and where Mr. Sanh's began. They were almost a single spirit, reunited.

Mr. Sanh held up a hand. "I must say, I feel a powerful force summoning us to cross over."

"Your murderer has been arrested, and you have been reunited with Con," I said. "You no longer have a reason to remain on earth."

Mr. Sanh nodded "You are wise beyond your years, young lady." He raised a hand goodbye. "Again, thank you all, so very much."

Con barked twice, then snuggled into Mr. Sanh.

"Con and I will be waiting for you."

I watched them lift away through tear-filled eyes.

Sonny told Grandpa what Mr. Sanh said. I was too emotional to speak.

Postscript

Saturday afternoon:

Mrs. Pidgeon said goodbye to the last student as he left the school library. The chair squeaked when she sat down at her desk to work on next week's lesson plans. Then, quiet. Total quiet.

A single crisp 'ping' broke the silence.

Mrs. Pidgeon's whole body jerked alert.

She dropped her pen, then lunged toward the right hand corner of the desk and snatched up the Astrobian radio transmitter.

She rotated it in her hand, took a breath and tapped the call button twice.

It had been twenty-seconds and she still hadn't let out her breath.

"Hello. Aunt Marge?"

Mrs. Pidgeon exhaled, "Pidge! Is this really you?"